Along for the Ride

A novel by

Mickey Royal

Along For The Ride

Library of Congress Cataloging-in-Publication Data is available upon request.

Manufactured in the United States of America
Cover Model: Gorgeous
Cover Layout: Cristina Gallegos
Bootstrap, Inc. (310) 387-7017

Published by:
Sharif Media

Table of Contents

Dedication

To: My Master Sijo Steve Muhammad, founder of the B.K.F. and Wu Shur Shin Chuan Fa System who imbedded the warrior spirit into me at an early age. It's still there.

To: My son Hussain Malik Sharif, who I love unconditionally. My past will never be your future.

To: My Mother whom I made so tired.
I never meant to cause you any pain or frustration. Thank you for loving me no matter how hard I made it at times.

To: Michael Esposito (Gentlemen's Video) a man of respect. My friend, my mentor, now and forever, you are appreciated.

Authors Note

This book is written in a style called Faction (Fact/Fiction). Certain facts have been omitted and events have been slightly altered in order to keep innocent people from being murdered.

Any killings discussed have to have already been solved or be public or street knowledge because there is no statue of limitations on murder. I have never and will never say or write anything that will incriminate myself or any of my friends, relatives or even enemies.

Acknowledgments

I wish to acknowledge the sacrifices my mother has made for me and my wellbeing. Thank you, mother, for constantly correcting my English when I spoke. I've been fortunate in my life to have had good friends, mentors and family. Vicki Gordon, Joanne Freeman, Marcus Garvey Elementary, Nettles Academy, Jasiri Williams, D-Smoove, Dorian Richie, Coze the Grinch, Eddie Goodman, Hussain Sharif, The Great Elephant Leslie Mohammed (R.I.P.), Imam Hamza, Ali Shakur, Vanessa Facen (R.I.P), George Washington Prep high school, Lucy Gordon, Abdullah Bin-Yahya, The Guru Dan Poynter, Donald Bakeer, Raquel Ramsey, Stacie Foote, Reg Frechette of Short Run Solutions, Chitose Freeman, Cheyanne Foxx, Janet Sharif, Master Sijo Steve (Papa) Muhammad founder of the B.K.F and Wu Shur Shin Chuan Fa, The N.O.I., Al-Ossrah, Michael Esposito, Grandmaster Lonzo, Lee Mack, International Lucky, Dr Richard Pozil, Dr Miguel Arias, Shawnte Andrews, Yolanda Allen, Mike Conception, Freeway Ricky Ross, Ron Hightower, New World Mafia (187 & 211 squads), and everyone else.

The writings of; Derek (Jack The Ripper) Marlowe, Richard (Slick Rick) Walters, Paul (Batman) Dini, Mustafa El-Amin & Neil Simon.

Foreword
By
Freeway Ricky Ross

What you are about to experience is a true phenomenon known as Mickey Royal. I've been privileged to have known him for many years. He's known in certain circles as a master teacher, an aristocrat of crime, a gangster, an all-around renaissance man, the premier writer of our time, a gentleman of leisure and true man of respect.

His story is legendary. I became a Mickey Royal fan after reading his first book The Pimp Game while in prison. Now the world will know how the legend began and its impact on current society.

As a young gangster growing up in Los Angeles California the work he put in has been verified and documented in many circles, trust me.

The term "The Real Deal" can only be applied to few people I've met in my lifetime and Mickey Royal is one of them. As a legend in the game myself, you can take my word for it. He is not to be taken lightly. I'm already on pins and needles waiting on another Mickey Royal novel.

Mickey Royal

To my Readers

I appreciate your patronage as well as your loyalty to my books. You incarcerated readers in particular have been my inspiration. I respect your unique position and I demand all of my books to be shipped first class, and within72 hours upon receiving payment.

Furthermore, I was so tired of pseudo intellectuals writing books about a lifestyle they've never lived, but insisting on passing themselves off as experts and expecting us to be too stupid to know the difference. Thank you for knowing the difference.

Thank You all for supporting me at www.mickeyroyal.com and on Facebook and Twitter.

Respectfully Yours

Mickey Royal

Chapter One

1992/Respect

So there I was, tired, bored but cool. Sunday night or should I say Monday morning, 1:41am., I'm sitting in a 1984 Buick Regal acting as lookout for two of my closest friends, Lamont Carlson and Antonio Brooks. They're inside the home of a so-called jeweler. The reason I say so-called is because the tip came from Chris Goods, and if you know Chris, you'd know his tips were half fact and half-exaggerated bullshit.

In my pocket, I had a dollar seventeen and two postage stamps. In my lap I had a Rossi .38 Special. I wasn't nervous, even though they had been in the house 30 minutes and the limit was 10. I was so tired. I've been in the life since age 14. By the time I was 18 years old I had seventy thousand dollars under my mattress. I drove a Nissan Maxima and I was a senior in high school.

Now at 20, two years, three girlfriends and four business ventures later, here I am. Flat broke with nothing but an impressive reputation on the street for shit I did that I can't even remember.

2:30a.m.

Up pulls the owner of the house. He makes eye contact with me and reaches into his glove compartment. Now I'm nervous. Being a street veteran, I knew with Antonio and Lamont inside I had to move. I started the car, got out and quickly approached the guy, gun drawn. He had in his left hand a metal cash box. In his right hand he had a cell phone. I put my .38 against his head and ran him from his driveway into his house.
Antonio saw the jeweler, punched him and asked; "Where is it"?

The jeweler handed him the cash box. Lamont came from downstairs, up to the main floor, and yelled that he had found a safe. He was sweating and excited. We, Antonio and I, took the jeweler downstairs and he opened the safe. Inside he had what appeared to be at least 10 grand and some jewelry.

Antonio took that too, and all four of us walked outside. We put the jeweler in the trunk of his own car and we got in mine, which was still running. This was sloppy, but a score none the less. We drove straight to Lamont's aunt's house, where he lived, to count and divide the loot.

We went upstairs to his room. Antonio dumped everything on the bed. I personally counted the cash; Eighty-two hundred in cash and some jewelry, which neither of us had any idea of its value. I told Lamont to hook up with Chris and see if he knows a fence.

Lamont said "Man, I can't. I'll be with my aunt all day tomorrow." I knew that was a cop out. He was scared of Chris because he was the nephew of Muhammad Salaam a.k.a. Big Momo.

Big Momo was in his mid-fifties and as hard as they came. He was connected and all blood and guts. He was an ex-Black Panther, ex-con, Vietnam Vet. He did over ten years for murder. In prison he formed an Islamic gang called Al-Ossrah, which means "The Family" in Arabic. The Press calls them The Muslim Mafia. Narcotics, extortion and gambling on the west side were controlled by Momo. Even Crips and Bloods wouldn't dare fuck with his action.

So, I took the jewelry and left Lamont's house. I dropped Antonio off at home and then I went home. I knew I would have to be the one to see Momo.

Lamont Carlson was a mama's boy, born with money and into a good family, but his need to belong led him to a gang life. Antonio Brooks was a ladies' man, smooth to the core. He's the type of man who wears a black silk suit to break into a house. He was a natural born hustler. He had a knack for finding a good score.

And there's me, Mikail Sharif, a Muslim and ex-gangster. I was hoping Momo and I could connect on the Islamic issue. I finally laid down to go to sleep after pacing with anxiety for two hours. The sun was up. It was 8:00a.m.

I woke up at 7:10p.m. and called Chris. I told him what was up and he said to come through around 9:30p.m. and he'll take me to see his uncle. I put on my black and white Stacy Adams. I had on my black slacks, black silk shirt, black trench coat and black fedora. I had to pick up Chris. Chris's uncle was Momo and yet Chris didn't own a car. I couldn't understand it.

I got to Chris's house at 9:00p.m. He came outside dressed like he was going to the beach. Here I was trying to make a good impression and he had on shorts and a tank top. He plopped in the Regal smelling like Brut cologne. He said, "Let's go, Bro." I didn't like him and he didn't like me and it was obvious. I resented having to work for/with an inferior in every way.

He knew that I looked down on him and he could feel my disrespect and disgust for him. At the same time, he could sense my feeling of being trapped and at his mercy. He knew by being Momo's nephew that he held more authority on the street and he could back it with proven results from "his boys", Lamont, Antonio and Mikail (Me). In this car, Chris knew that he held the power, and whenever I forgot, he reminded me.

We pulled up to the street and my stomach was in knots. Momo lived at the end of a cul-de-sac in Ladera Heights, a neighborhood where affluent Black families live. I parked across the street and Chris's fake smile, which appears to be painted on at times, was gone. This was serious. Something appeared to be going on when we arrived. The garage door was open and the garage was filled with free weights.

As we walked up to the garage, Sasquatch, Momo's live-in bodyguard, told us to wait.
I stopped in my tracks like a robot and so did Chris. Chris then asked if Momo was home. Sasquatch

replied by saying, "Yes, Mr. Salaam is in. I'll see if he's in the mood for company." Sasquatch stood 6 feet 9 inches with 350-400lbs of muscle. He was visually intimidating. He had no mustache but a full beard. He had one lazy eye and two missing front teeth.

Momo came out with him and I had goose bumps all over my body. Sasquatch was watching my every move. Momo was well groomed with a salt and pepper goatee. His head was bald and he resembled Hawk from the TV series, Spencer for Hire. He stood about 5 feet 10 inches. He stared at me until my eyes blinked and then he said,

"As- Salaam Alaikum"

"Wa-Alaikum Salaam." I replied with confidence.

He asked my name. I said Mikail Sharif. He introduced himself as Muhammad Salaam, as if I didn't already know who he was. He told me to pick his daughters up from Southwest Jr. College with Chris and we'll discuss my future tomorrow.

I asked Mr. Salaam "What about the jewelry?"

He answered,

"What jewelry?"

I had gotten out of my place by speaking so Chris quickly pushed me out of the door and said that we'll be right back.

We arrived at Southwest at 10:10pm. They got out at 10:00pm and had been waiting for ten minutes. His daughters were 19 years old. Beautiful twin girls, Aminah and Fatimah, total opposites. Fatimah was what you might call a daddy's girl. She was dressed in hijab traditionally Islamic from head to toe. Totally covered but stylish. Aminah had on jeans, a tube top and heels, with her hair styled and had on plenty of make-up with an attitude to match.

As soon as they got in the car, Aminah started in on me. "Who the fuck is this, Chris who is your friend?"

"Mikail" he replied.

"Buy him a fucking watch." Fatimah interrupted and said "As-Salaam Alaikum" and I replied "Wa-Alaikum Salaam." She then asked if I could turn up the heat. So I did. She leaned back and stared out of the window, trying to ignore her sister who just wouldn't shut up. I held my tongue all of the way back to Momo's. Aminah and Chris had some sort of bond going back to their childhood. She and he were loud and offensive all the way back to Momo's.

We pulled up in the driveway and Chris and I walked the girls to the front door. Chris walked them inside and told me to wait on the porch. He came out ten minutes later with a look on his face like the cat that swallowed the canary. On the way home Chris told me that I was to meet with Momo at 12 noon sharp at M&M's. M & M's was a soul food restaurant on Crenshaw and King Blvd. I had realized after dropping Chris off that the purpose of the meeting had nothing to do with the sale of the jewelry. When I got home, the first thing I did was check my answering machine. Lamont and Antonio had left several messages on my machine about the jewelry. But I called Antonio back first.

I called him and explained to him what had happened. He couldn't hear the rest of the conversation because he was ecstatic about Momo and me having a face-to-face meeting. He wanted to know details. There we were like two teenage cheerleaders gossiping about the husky captain of the football team. I asked Antonio what he thought Momo wanted from me.

Antonio was so excited. He immediately called Lamont on three-way so that he, too, could hear the good news. He did so right when I was about to talk about the jewelry. I wanted to talk to him, just Antonio, first. He called Lamont because we're a crew I guess.

I personally would have preferred to tell them one at a time. Now we're all on three-way. Lamont asked me off the bat. "Where's the money from the jewelry? How much did we get?" I explained to them that I still had the goods and that Chris never told Momo about the jewels. Lamont was furious because he had undoubtedly blown his money from the score.

Antonio knew what a face-to-face meeting meant with Momo. Lamont, never seeing the big picture, didn't understand the value of a connection like Momo's. I told them both that I had no idea what Momo wanted, but it had nothing to do with jewelry. I told Lamont that the jewelry may be worth about twenty grand. I also told him that if he was so broke that he couldn't wait until I moved it that I would loan him $500. He said I'm on my way over to get it and then he quickly hung up. Antonio had remained silent while Lamont and I had talked. Now Antonio told me "Good luck tomorrow Cuz". He asked me if I needed back up. I said that such a move would be an insult to Momo. If Momo wanted to harm me, I'd been already harmed.

Antonio was now bugging me about another score. He wasn't broke, just looking for action. Plus, just how long does $2,500 last these days on the street? So I made up my mind that whatever Momo had on his mind, I was game.

The answer was yes to whatever he asked.

The Meeting

I showed up at M&M's early to see Momo arrive. He pulls up alone in a black convertible Bentley. Leimert Park was his area and everybody knew it. He was loved and best known for his ex-Panther days rather than his more current role as King Momo, the Crime Boss. Even though the community knows what he does there's still a high level of respect for him. Momo's the real deal.

He sat down in front of me and greeted me again with As-Salaam Alaikum and I stood as he sat and answered WA-Alaikum Salaam, sir. He told me that he knew about me. He stated that he knew about the banks and supermarkets that I had done. "Impressive. I know that you've put in your share of work. You're also a Muslim," he said.

I listened to Momo as he spoke to me about me. I didn't interrupt.

"Chris tells me you keep your head in any situation and you know when to keep your mouth shut. Dig it. Did you meet my daughters, Fatimah and

Aminah?" I told him yes, that I really remember Aminah. She had given me a hard time. He remained expressionless, ignored my comment and continued. He told me that on Monday, I was to register for these classes at Southwest College.

He slid me a list of classes, teachers and the time and day. He told me that these times we live in are dangerous times. "Mikail, you're the same age of the students at Southwest. I want you to keep a close eye on my babies. You'll pick them up. You'll have the same classes and schedule as they do. You'll walk them to the front door. Ali will take it from there."

"Ali?"

He paused, took a deep breath, exhaled and said, "Sasquatch."

He pushed me an envelope and got up and left. The way he moved, the way he spoke, I could tell clearly that he was not offering, he was ordering.

Al-Ossrah is a powerful religious organized crime family. They had 99 members (symbolic of Allah's 99 attributes).

They always had only 99 members, no more, no less. New members were let in only if old members died, and that was seldom. The ninety-nine didn't play. Their average age was over 40.

These were grown men, ex-Vietnam vets, ex-Black Panthers, and ex-B.L.A. Some were ex-cons, with a militant Islamic fundamentalist air about them. They usually recruited in prison or from the mosques. Al-Ossrah currently exists with two leaders, one inside, one outside.

I was starting to see the game unfold. He was auditioning me for membership. Al-Ossrah had no youth in its organization. I could tell Momo was scared. He had young competition coming up in the bordering sets. The Rolling Sixties Crip Gang and Black P. Stone Nation Blood Gang were both looking to make a major move in narcotics. It wasn't wartime yet, but times were tense, mainly because both gangs had thousands of members.

I opened up the envelope and inside was a note and ten one hundred-dollar bills.

The note read;

Chris told me about the jewelry. Go to Diamond's Pawn Shop on Central Avenue in Watts. Tell him Momo sent you and give him any jewelry you might have. Diamond will help you.

I went to Diamond. He was extremely rude and short with me. I showed him the jewels and he gave me five grand in small bills. I thanked him and said Mr. Salaam said that you were fair. He caught me at the door and pulled me into the back. He gave me an additional $10,000 and told me the jewels were worth a little over $30,000. Mr. Diamond told me next time mention that you're with Mr. Salaam. On my way out, he said, "Give my Salaams to Mr. Salaam."

Benjamin Diamond was an old Jew. He and Muhammad went way back to the Black Panther/civil rights days. They met in Vietnam and have been close friends ever since. Benjamin has had his pawn shop in Watts since the 60's. Right after the Watts riots Ben was one of those Jews who fought for civil rights. When Muhammad went to prison, it was Ben Diamond and the Diamond family who worked with the parole board for his release.

So now I had a job and $16,000 in my pocket. I went to Antonio's house first and gave him three grand from the jewels. Then I went to Lamont's house and gave him three grand also.

Lamont bitched, moaned and complained about the amount. He talked all kinds of shit about me and Momo getting close and that I'm thinking I'm a big shot. He went on and on and I just left while he was still complaining.

Antonio was too busy going to barber school to be bothered with details. Lamont, who had no hustling street survival skills, was literally jealous at how close to Momo I had gotten. He was feeling threatened. He wanted a chance to prove himself. I felt as though I was doing all of the work, so I kept 9 grand from the jewelry for myself.

Now at school Monday morning, I discovered that I was pre-registered. Apparently Momo's connections go past the streets.

So, there I was babysitting the Salaam twins. I have my head down doing classwork, so it seems. But actually, I had on a small, thin, bulletproof vest, hidden by my black t-shirt and jacket.

My backpack was in front of my seat, resting on my left foot. In it I had my .38 snub nose revolver. I kept the top open for easy entry and kept my eyes open. The twins sat directly in front of me.

Aminah hated being followed by me. We told the other students that I was their cousin. Fatimah was in school to pass the time but Aminah was in the transfer program. So the three of us walked around the campus together.

For the first two weeks it was cool. I was being paid a thousand dollars every week to watch two of the most beautiful sisters I've ever seen. Fatimah was the type of woman I could see myself being married to in the future. Aminah was growing tired of me.

One day after about a month or so, it just hit the fan. The tension between Aminah and I had built up and had come to a head.

She kept wanting to hang around this wild crowd of girls.

Fatimah wanted to go to the library to study for our test. I told Aminah that I couldn't watch both of them at the same time in different places. Aminah told me that she didn't need anybody to watch her. She told me that she was grown. She and I argued right there in the hallway.

I guess the stress of a dead mother and a gangster father got to her. She snatched away from me. I then grabbed her by the arm. Not to my surprise, she knew martial arts and gave me a swift kick to the groin. I went down on one knee and before I knew it, I had leaped up and pimp slapped(back-hand) Aminah, knocking her off her feet. Reality hit me twice as hard as I hit her. I knew that I was dead now. Since I played that card, I just decided to continue.

"I work for Mr. Salaam. He doesn't own me, and you don't own me either."

She screamed "Stay the fuck away from me!" Then she took off running. Fatimah told me to relax.

She said that Aminah will come around. I was thrilled to see Aminah in our next class. Somehow that slapping incident brought all three of us closer. We were all becoming prisoners in this street war shit.

I could announce all I wanted about my independence and strength, but the truth was, I was trapped too.

Lamont, Antonio and I had drifted since I had become Mr. Salaam's flunky. I hated following these girls around, to the mall, to school, to the movies, etc. Even though we had become closer, all three of us were tired of it and each other. Mr. Salaam was treating me like a son now because his daughters were treating me like a brother.

On the street I could see and feel the jealousy between the members of Al-Ossrah and myself. I was not a full-fledged member yet and charter members weren't as close to Momo as I was. Among the jealous was a 36-year-old soldier named Mustafa.

Chapter Two

Mustafa

One evening, after I had walked the girls to the door, I went to Shabazz Restaurant, a Muslim restaurant where Ossrah soldiers were known to hang out. I was eating a slice of bean pie and feeling strong for the first time in my life. I had 15 grand stashed away and I was being paid 4 grand a month to hang out. Just when I was feeling on top of the world, in comes Mustafa.

Mustafa was a fearless psychopath who had a blood lust equal to that of a vampire. Sasquatch described him as "not playing with a full deck". Even more than murder or money, Mustafa lusted for power. He walks in and points at me with his right index finger and says, "Sharif, come with me."

The right index finger has a gold wedding band on it. The right index finger is the finger that remains held during a Shahada. All members of Al-Ossrah have this ring on that finger. I do not have a ring.

This was his way of reminding me of this. To add insult to injury, Mustafa was a Sheikh (lieutenant). In the chain of command of Al-Ossrah it went; Jamal the Sultan (Sultan was the highest rank in Al-Ossrah) who is serving life without possibility of parole and Momo, who was the Caliph second in command, but in complete control of the sect on the outside. Al-Ossrah had five Sheikhs, symbolic of the Five Pillars of Islam. Two are in prison, three on the streets. Each with a squad of ten to twenty-five soldiers under their command. Mustafa was a lieutenant who reported only to Jamal. He often butted heads with Momo. Mustafa had close ties with the heads of The Black Guerrilla Family, Al-Ossrah's closest allies.

This was the first time I had been alone with Mustafa. He had just gotten out of prison and drove

a new B.M.W. and had a fist full of C-notes.
The first thing he asked me was have you fucked Aminah yet. I didn't reply. He had a raspy voice and spoke crudely. He then said that she's a slut.
I paused and then asked him,
"So, what do you want with me?"
"We want you to set up shop at Southwest."
He was telling me to sell drugs at the school where Momo's daughters attended. This would be suicidal disrespect. I said
"Who is we?"
"Me and the Sultan."
He paused, made eye contact and then said Jamal.

Then he revealed something that no one else knew. He said that Momo has nothing to with narcotics just gambling and extortion. He shakes down independent dope dealers, pimps, strip clubs, and restaurants.10% from legit clubs, 35% from drug dealers, 20% from pimps and 5% from restaurants. If you multiply the areas under his control it adds up to a lot of money.

"What does this have to do with me?"

"Jamal is in the joint, we run narcotics and I am responsible for the Sultan's interest, not the Caliph's (Momo).

Mustafa wanted me to hook up with some cat named Mississippi Slick. Mustafa was not an ex-Panther or anything like that. He was straight from the prison psych ward. Mustafa became a member in prison but even before then he had already been known as a heavy-duty soldier with The El-Rukns out of Chicago.

He put in a lot of work and moved up quickly, mainly because he shared a cell with Jamal for several years. A blind man could see what Mustafa wants and he let me know in so many words that he had the backing of Jamal. Jamal wasn't the man Momo was, but 1/4 of Al-Ossrah is in prisons across the states and so is Jamal.

We, Mustafa and I, met with Mississippi Slick. He had a stolen car ring. He was in charge of a group of cats from the south that stole cars and drove them to Mexico, register them and bring them back to sell below blue book value on used car lots. Slick was an independent outsider who did what he wanted. But this is L.A. and you can't operate in this city without backing and Mustafa backed him one hundred percent.

Slick would also steal cars and buy junk cars the same year, color, make and model. He'd register the junk and then switch the VIN numbers with the stolen cars. He had it down to a science. Slick's crew had this operation down to the smallest detail. The operation brought in 100 grand a week on the average. This meant 20% each week for Al-Ossrah with 5 % going to Mustafa personally.1% a week for each of Mustafa's crew members, leaving 3 % each week for Jamal personally.

Momo got nothing from this. In addition to setting up shop at Southwest, Mustafa was also now putting me in charge of collecting the 20% from Slick. Thus the purpose of meeting Slick.

Slick was cool. He had the demeanor of an accountant. He wore round horn-rimmed glasses and carried a briefcase.

He had a gap between his teeth. But his suits don't fool me. Slick was just a car thief who went to business school and had successfully combined them both. Slick had the nerve to be living in Leimert Park, Momo's hood. Slick wasn't from around here and he was not a gangster. He spoke with a heavy southern accent.

Mustafa asked me how much is Momo paying me?

"Four grand a month."

Mustafa laughed and peeled off two grand and said every Monday when you pick up our cut, take your cut off of the top. Mustafa was offering me two grand a week, but why? I had no intentions of cutting Momo out, but even I was not crazy enough to disagree with Mustafa in front of him. I took his money, played along and the next day I took the twins to school.

The semester was coming to a close. We were a tight clique now. Today we decided to play hookey and go to the beach. Fatimah, always a class act, had her hair and body covered. She had on flats, plus a one-piece bathing suit with a body wrap tied around her waist. This was wild for her.

We played music, mostly rap and relaxed on the sand. Aminah had on a two-piece thong and she looked delicious. She ran to the water and dove into the wave, which knocked her back. We all laughed. Aminah trotted back to the water and started screaming, "Mikail come in with me!"

Fatimah and I were laughing. This beach trip took off some of the stress. It was Friday. We left the beach and picked up Chris and went on to Disneyland.

"What will your father think about the beach and Disneyland?"

"He's not even in the country. He's always gone like ten days each month" said Aminah.

We had a blast at Disneyland. I dropped Chris off at about 1:00am. Fatimah was asleep in the car. We all went to my apartment. We watched videos and played checkers til all three of us got sleepy. I told them that it was now time to go. I was having a hard time staying awake. I drove them both home as usual. I went back to my apartment and took a shower and went to bed.

The next morning, or should I say six hours later, I got a knock on my window. It was Aminah. I let her in. I told her she should be home today because it was Saturday. She had on jeans, a tank top and a leather jacket with a pair of black boots.

"What's up, how'd you get here?"

"I drove my dad's Harley. I can do a lot of things if given some space."

Then she asked if I were married. I told her that I'm 21. We stood there looking at each other, continuing the conversation.

I leaned forward to kiss her and she met me halfway. We were locked in a passionate kiss at the door and she started licking my neck as I was undressing in the doorway. I picked her up piggyback from the front and took her to my bedroom. She wasn't a virgin.

Before I knew it, I was inside of her. This was the first woman I had touched in months, since I had started working for Momo. She was also the first woman I had ever made love to. I've had sex, but I was in love for the first time.

We were in my room for hours. Aminah was screaming my name, scratching my back.

When we finished, we took a shower together. She put on one of my shirts and a pair of my socks and got on my phone. I went to the kitchen and overheard her conversation.

"Ali, I'm going to be at Mikail's until Sunday. If you need me, call me." I then asked her if she was trying to get me killed.

"Reeelaaaxxx, Squatch is cool like that."

"What if he tells your father?"

"My father knows I fuck." Then she elaborated when she noticed the shocked look on my face brought on by her language.

She told me that her sister chooses to wait until she's married, she doesn't. "All you Muslim brothers are always preaching this shit about the little virgin Muslim wife who knows her place, who sits at home, cooks, cleans, has babies and shuts up. My mother was like that.

Fatimah acts just like Mama."

Aminah then asked me how many virgin Muslim brothers I knew.

"What does your father say?"

"My father is a drug dealer. Do you think his fucking opinion matters to me? I'm sure Allah is more concerned with my dad's contribution to the destruction of the community as opposed to my sexual appetite." The next thing I knew, she was sitting on my lap, kissing me.

The doorbell rang, it was Antonio. I introduced them to each other. She asked him if he wanted something to eat or drink because she was about to make breakfast. Antonio told her no thank you and pulled me outside and said

"Nigga, what are you doing?"

"What?"

"That's Momo's daughter."

"Duh"

I asked him how he knew who she was. He showed me the license plate on the Harley that read 'Momo

4'. I took this time to gloat. I was fucking Momo's daughter and getting paid by Momo and Mustafa.

I threw this in Antonio's face, not being mean, but just feeling good. While Antonio and I were outside, we heard the vacuum cleaner going. Even though this was the first time we had made love, we were extremely close already. We had become friends first.

Antonio was giving me the street gossip. He was always good for that. He was telling me that he was doing his rap music thing now full time and cutting hair. He said that he now only did scores when he was broke. I asked Antonio if he was okay for bread. He was okay, but I gave him a grand anyway and asked about Lamont. I was informed that Lamont was selling dope with some Watts Crip niggas and that Lamont was coming up. Antonio told me that his rap name was Tony Pleasure, which was also becoming his street name. Tony was cool. I liked him.

When I went back in the house, Aminah was on the phone with a woman who had called for me.

After the things Aminah said, I'm sure that woman wouldn't be calling again.

I didn't ask who it was and I didn't care.

Monday Morning:

I picked up the girls as usual for school and Aminah got in and kissed me. I asked Fatimah how was her weekend. She cut her eyes at me and just stared out of the window. She was angry because Aminah and I were having relations. As the day went on, Fatimah started to talk to me and the clique was tight once more.

My pager was going off all day. It was Slick. I felt so guilty inside. I knew that I had to make a choice. I went to a phone booth and called Momo. I told him that I had to see him today. He could tell by the sound of my voice that I was troubled. He asked about the girls. I told him that they were fine. I told him that I had a much bigger problem.

That night when I dropped off the girls, I told Momo about that day with Mustafa. He looked out of his window on his patio and told me to ride with him. He went into the back and came out with a briefcase. We took his Mercedes, I drove. He said he was going to meet this Mississippi Slick personally. I was truly nervous now. I didn't trust Mustafa or like him. I really didn't want to be in the middle of anything like this, but my first loyalty was to Mr. Salaam.

We pulled up at the garage Slick was leasing and working out of. He had close to twenty grand waiting in a brown paper bag for me to deliver to Mustafa.

"What's up my Nigga? Is this your Benz, he said?" Slick had no idea who Momo was. I discovered later that apparently, I didn't either.

Momo told me to get the bag. I turned around to get the bag and by the time I turned back around, Slick was dead. Momo had stabbed him in the stomach, spun his body around, lifted his chin and slit his throat in one motion just that fast.

Momo calmly got into the Benz while the money and I hopped in quickly.

Slick's boys were thieves, not killers. They ran as Slick's body dropped. For the first time since I had met Mr. Salaam, I saw him with clear vision. Momo was a gangster. I was no rookie to the streets. This was war. These were real gangsters, with real guns and real bullets.

Mr. Salaam placed a call on the cell phone and told Sasquatch one word, "Dawah," then hung up. When we pulled up in the driveway, there were about thirty brothers. They were muscular, in all black and strategically holding post up and down the street. There were cars everywhere. The garage door was up and about ten soldiers were in the garage and twenty or so soldiers were out in front. None were in the house.

When Mr. Salaam and I walked in the house, I tried to give him the bag. He ignored me and called for Aminah and Fatimah to come downstairs. They each had one suitcase. The girls seemed to be accustomed to this.

They looked so tired of the bullshit. Momo told me to take the bag and the girls to my house. He wanted us to continue to go to school. He figured if the girls lives weren't disrupted too much he could then keep a good hold on his gang and his family.

I rushed the girls to my car, and we left. Mustafa was paging me, putting in 187 in my pager. 187 is the LAPD code for murder.

On the way home I noticed that we were being followed. I slowed down to let him catch up. The car pulled on the side of us and I saw a guy wave to me. While I tried to place his face, I heard Fatimah let out an ear-piercing scream. The backseat passenger had his hand pointed at her face. In his hand was a 9mm Beretta semi-automatic pistol. Both Aminah and Fatimah ducked down as I stepped on the gas, then slammed on the brakes.

As the gunmen sped past us, the backseat passenger fired 5 shots, two breaking through the front windshield. Aminah tried to exit the car and as I saw the car coming back, I told Aminah to stay in the car, stay down and trust me.

All I had was that .38 revolver with five shots. I got out of the car and hid behind a car parked behind my Buick. Both gunmen got out of their car and ran up to the Buick, both with guns drawn.

I came from behind the car and with two shots, I dropped one gunman point blank range in the chest. The other gunman ran back to the car.

I ran across the street after him, putting one in his back. I ran back to the Buick and took off. We were obviously followed from Momo's house. I went to Tony Pleasure's apartment instead of my place. I felt that he could be trusted.

We parked down the street, got out and walked up to his building. Tony wasn't home, but I had a set of his keys. Fatimah started going through his refrigerator and began to make everyone sandwiches, with chips and soda.

Aminah was curled up on the sofa, in shock no doubt. I assumed that Mustafa probably had some soldiers outside of my house. I also knew I couldn't call the old gang from Inglewood because with Mustafa's money, he's put the word out with them too. Gang love is one thing, but money talks and Mustafa has plenty. Tony was the only one I felt could help us. We, the girls and I, were in the middle of an internal gang war. Al-Ossrah seemed to be at war with itself.

Tony came home and wasn't surprised to see us. I told Tony that I needed to use his car. He said okay but wanted to know why. I told him that Mustafa's people know my car but I can sneak home and get my money and be back if I had a different car.

I directed him to stay with the girls and to guard them with his life. Tony told me about two niggas who had gotten killed off Crenshaw tonight. He said that cops and helicopters were everywhere. I just played stupid. I trusted Tony, but still, you never know.

I lived off of Crenshaw on 111th Street. I drove to 110th Street. I parked right in front of the house that sits behind the apartment complex I live in. I went through the yard and went through my bathroom window that was always open.

The window faced an alley so no one saw me break in. I went to my safe and it hadn't been touched. I got my 15 grand out of the safe and headed back out of the window. I didn't look but I'm sure some guys were waiting for me out front.

I hopped in Tony's car and drove back to his place. When I walked through the door, Aminah leaped into my arms and gave me a big kiss. Now I had thirty-five grand and Momo's daughters. I had two bullets left in my .38 which I would give to Tony to destroy later. We didn't go to school anymore of course. We just stayed in Tony's apartment day after day.

Tony came in one night looking like he had seen a ghost. He asked me to step outside to talk. He showed me the newspapers. The local papers followed the gangs in L.A. as if they were football teams in some sort of tournament. The front page read "Changing of the Guard." Another paper read, "Reap What You Sow." The war was over. Muhammad Abdul Salaam, along with two other soldiers, had been gunned down. Mr. Salaam was killed as he slept in his bed.

When I walked bsck in Aminah asked, "Baby, what's for dinner?"

"When can we go home? Have you at least talked to my father?" asked Fatimah.

I didn't soften the blow or sugarcoat it. I told them that Mr. Salaam was dead, that he had been killed. I tossed both newspapers on the table for them to see for themselves. Fatimah ran to Tony's bedroom in tears and Aminah plopped down on the couch and tried to hold it in. Mustafa was now in control of the soldiers on the outside and Jamal ran the inside. No one has seen Sasquatch since the murders. He's wanted for questioning by F.B.I. and L.A.P.D.

I told Aminah and Fatimah that we should separate. Mustafa is pissed at me, not you.
"Do you have somewhere to go?"
They said that they had an aunt in Fremont, California. They repacked their one bag each, made a phone call to their Aunt Sylvia and we left for the

train station.

On the way, Aminah told me she wanted to stay with me, wherever I go, she wanted to go. Tony drove us to the train station. I bought three one-way tickets for Fremont and we left.
Before leaving, I gave Tony five grand cash and thanked him.
Then we left...

On the train ride up north we just sat together quietly. We rode first class all together in our own separate sleepers. I figured the girls needed some privacy and I needed to think. I didn't know what to expect of this war stuff. All I knew if given another chance, gunmen wouldn't miss. I didn't know who to trust, but I trusted the Salaam girls.

They both looked at me as if I was all they had and I could hear Momo saying "Protect my girls." I kept hearing his voice over and over and like a knight who had sworn a blood oath to his king I was going to follow orders, no matter what the cost.

Chapter Three

Five Years in Fremont

Adjusting to Fremont was easier for the girls than for me. I didn't know that Aminah was pregnant before we came up here and her Aunt Sylvia insisted we get married. She was originally from Memphis, Tennessee and was a southern woman at heart. She made us sleep in separate rooms until we were married, so we got married. We were now Mikail and Aminah Sharif, the newlyweds. Fatimah had met and become attached to a Sunni Muslim brother named Hassan. He was courting her and very respectful. Aminah, Fatimah and I had joined the local mosque and were trying to become an active part of our community.

After the first two months, Aminah and I moved out and found an apartment. A lovely two-bedroom place overlooking Hwy 880. I gave Aunt Sylvia three hundred bucks a month even after we moved out to pay for Fatimah's rent, food and other expenses. I appreciated everything Sylvia had done for us in the wake of her brother-in-law's death. Especially helping us to get better adjusted to our new surroundings, I really appreciated her for that.

Aminah and I were playing house. She was now nine months pregnant and ready to deliver any minute. I had bought a used Ford Taurus sedan cash. I had about 18 grand left and we were happy. The baby's room was all made up for him.

Aminah was a daddy's girl. She was raised with money all of her life. She was used to Jamaica and Cancun vacations twice a year. She wore a watch that her father sent to Switzerland to get repaired. She had no true concept of our situation as she planned her next shopping spree with our stash.

I had no job and no skills. I had never done anything but hustled on the streets. Fremont was a suburb and I saw very little action coming or going. I had checked out Oakland for some action. I couldn't change what I was.

I was a hustler and a man, and men work. Even though we had money, I was feeling less of a man because I was not generating any income. How long could our money last? Rent, utilities, food, baby expenses.

September 24, 1993, our son was born. Hussain Malik Sharif, our son. The baby brought us closer, but we were still young 22 and 20-year olds.

I finally found work at a warehouse, loading and unloading trucks. Aminah was anemic and always tired. For some reason she refused to take her iron pills. She claimed they made her constipated. When my son turned one, our fights began. We had pissed through our money and I could no longer afford our rent working for $7.50 per hour. I had no choice but to get another full-time job. I was working from 6:00am to 2:30pm, then from 3:00pm to midnight, five days a week. Aminah's spoiled princess attitude had been buried.

She was now bitter, mean spirited and constantly shouting profanities at our child. She would lash out at the both of us out of frustration due to our new financial situation. I had to take the car to work everyday because she was too tired or lazy to drop me off at work. She was just frustrated from being stuck in the house all day everyday with a one year old.

On the weekends I would just sit in front of the TV on the couch with Aminah in my arms and talk about the Southwest College days in L.A. We would both constantly talk about going back but how? We had no extra cash and a baby now.

I kept in contact with Tony, and Aminah talked to Chris at least twice a month. Tony was in cosmetology school and writing songs. Chris was busy asking Aminah where her father hid his money, which hadn't been found. Fatimah had grown more and more distant by this time. She was married to Hassan and they were doing well.

Hassan's father owned an auto-body repair shop which Hassan managed and was soon to take over partial ownership. Fatimah enjoyed being a housewife and they made a good team. When Aminah and Fatimah would talk on the phone I would hear the envy in Aminah's voice. She would usually be depressed after she and her sister talked. She would then lash out at the baby or attempt to pick an argument with me.

Hassan had the things Aminah wanted. He owned an Infinity Q45 and a Range Rover and Fatimah didn't even know how to drive. She was content just walking to the corner grocery store everyday to select fresh vegetables for that night's dinner. She always grocery shopped for one day only.

Everybody in her neighborhood knew and liked her. They lived in a three-bedroom, two bath town house. They were trying to have a baby but had not yet been successful.

By this time Hussain was three and Aminah just flipped. She began wearing short skirts and hanging out with a fast crowd. She would drop Hussain off with her sister and be gone for days.

One night on my lunch break from my second job, I went to the nightclub where she and her new friends hung out. I walked in and saw her at the bar between two guys and she was drinking. She didn't see me, so I just left. I had suspected her of cheating all along but I needed proof. I needed closure.

One day when I was on lunch break from my first job. I saw another car parked in my parking stall. I came in and I could hear her moaning and calling out his name. I could hear him spanking her and asking, "Whose is it?" She was screaming back his name, "David!"

I stood outside the door until they finished and he opened the door. I hit him and started choking him. Aminah ran to call the cops screaming, "He's crazy!" I beat him until the cops pulled me off of him.

What happened next hurt worst than any bullet I have ever felt. Aminah told the cops that David was her boyfriend and I was the jealous ex-husband who no longer lived there.

She pressed assault charges and I was arrested. Before the car drove off, I saw her walk back into the house with David and my son.

I spent only 11 months and 29 days in jail but I was able to see clearly. For the first two nights I couldn't sleep. I just kept hearing her screams as she called out his name.

Fatimah came to visit me on a regular basis and put money on my books. We talked about Southwest College for a while, but mostly we talked about her sister. She told me that David was just some guy she had met at a club. He had told her what he could do for her if she went to Oakland with him and she believed him.

Fatimah always felt grateful for me saving her and her sister's lives and also for paying her rent when she lived with Sylvia. Fatimah was always offering me money now or favors. I asked her whether Aminah was still with David and where was my son. Fatimah said that all David wanted was some steady pussy for a while and now that he's got it, he's gone.

While in jail, I decided positively to go back to L.A. I told Fatimah that I had nothing here anymore.

"What about your son?"

"He's seen his share of drama and arguments. Besides, I'm losing up here. I have to be myself. I have to be a man. I can do more for them both back in Los Angeles."

When I got out of jail Fatimah, Aminah and my son Hussain were there to pick me up. Aminah was driving the Taurus and started in immediately. "The rent is due and I don't have it."

"Ask David for it" I told her. Fatimah was staring out of the window and patting my son on the leg.

The first day back I began to sleep on the couch. What hurt the most is that she took someone's side over mine. We never had sex or even kissed again. Fearing another incident Fatimah offered me a room in her and Hassan's home and so I moved out.

Hassan didn't mind and Fatimah knew with us being emotionally separated, we should be physically separated before one of us killed the other.

Aminah hated the fact that Fatimah was helping me. Fatimah and I made a deal. The deal was that I could live with her and Hassan rent-free only if I continued to pay half Aminah's rent. I agreed.

I lived with them for two years and saved close to $1,500. I let Aminah have the car. I packed my bags on April 20, 1997 and called the bus station to see when my bus would leave. I went by Aminah's to say goodbye to my son. Aminah was packing also because with me gone she wouldn't be able to afford the rent by herself. She would have to move in with Fatimah.

She and I gave each other a big hug. I felt guilty for leaving her with my baby by herself. I told her if she wanted to come to L.A., I would set her up with a job and an apartment once I got settled myself. She knew I still loved her, so she knew I wasn't just talking. I had seen it coming.

Aminah was easily influenced by the crowd

and she loved sex. It was bound to happen. Aminah was a follower. I gave her five-hundred dollars in her doorway, kissed my son and left. I took that lonely Greyhound bus ride by myself back to Los Angeles after being gone for five years. I couldn't help but wonder what had been going on in my absence. It felt weird going back alone.

Chapter Four

Monte Carlo

I told no one I was coming. When I first got to L.A. with two suitcases and a grand in my pocket I called Tony to pick me up. He was happy to see me when he arrived at the bus station.

"Where's the fam?"

"They'll be coming later, after I get set up."

"Where you are staying?"

"I was going to check into a motel for right now then hopefully rent a room from someone."

"No, you're staying with me."

We arrived at his place over in Compton. He lived in a one-bedroom apartment in Fruit Town Piru Hood. He was looking at me like I was Jesus who had been resurrected to save him. I told him that I was gonna look for a job tomorrow.

"A job? Yeah right, you? Nigga get dressed. We're gonna go roll on some ho's."

I took a shower, got dabbed up and we left.

He took me to a club on the west side in Gardena called Monte Carlo. It was a strip club. There was plenty of action coming in and out, from high-rollers to working-class Joes. While I was at the bar Tony went in the back of the club and came back out with Lamont.

I really didn't wish to dive back into the life this soon. I didn't feel like seeing anyone but it was too late. Lamont gave me a slow patronizing hug. Tony was showing me off like some kid showing off his famous father, the basketball player, at his elementary school.

"Lamont what's been up?" He corrected me with a frown on his face,

"It's Monte Brother, Monte Carlo." We all went to the VIP section and listened to him brag about his marijuana deals and his club. He was doing well.

He was really happy to see that I wasn't. He offered me a job as his driver, but I told him that I was okay.

"Where are you staying?"

"He's staying with me" interrupted Tony.

A lot can change in five years but to me "Monte" was still that crybaby momma's boy I grew up with. He could tell I felt so by the look in my eyes. When I saw the shit Monte had I wanted in. The streets never change but like tides in a mighty ocean, the power in the ghetto shifts constantly.

I tried my best to ignore the fact that Monte had a gold wedding band on his index finger. I knew he wasn't Islamic. He pointed that finger at me and said, "If you need me, call me." He then leaned forward, put his hand on my shoulder and whispered "I need a soldier like you." On the way home I kept hearing that word – soldier. I had no intentions on working for Lamont "Monte Carlo" Carlson. Maybe I was being jealous, but still I'm human and I had my pride.

11:35pm

The doorbell rang; it was a woman. Not just a woman, but the finest, sexiest woman I've ever seen. She stood a little over six feet. She was wearing a black trench coat and beautiful smile.
"I'm here to see Mick, Mick I,"
"Mikail."
"Whatever…Is that you?"
"Yes, but have we met?"

She walked in without being invited, opened her coat and said, "My name is Gorgeous. I dance at Monte Carlos." She was wearing black and gold sheer see through lingerie with clear high heals. She was the kind of woman men killed for, and died for.

"Are we alone?" I didn't answer. "Don't worry it's paid for" she said as she rubbed her right hand across her vagina. I told her I wasn't interested, that she could leave.

"Are you a fag or something?"

I grabbed her by her throat with my left hand and shoved her out of the door, then slammed it. I wasn't mad at her. I was still mad about Lamont. I was mad about my living situation, mad that he was high-rolling and I wasn't.

I waited until Tony came home and told him what had happened.

"Tony, how did Lamont get a ring?"

"Mustafa started a new gang called Black Mafia Hustlers. Anyone who turns a profit can join. Al-Ossrah went underground. Mustafa tells guys like Lamont if they earn him enough money then they can eventually buy membership into Black Mafia Hustlers and eventually become full fledged members of Al-Ossrah when it's time for new members."

"Tony, that all sounds like some bullshit.

Take me back up to that club tomorrow night."

The next night we went back up to Monte Carlo's. On the way there I tried to fathom Lamont with power. Tony was helping me as best he could. He'd cut hair in the day and go clubbing at night. He made good money and kept trying to offer me some, but I wouldn't take it.

When we got there Lamont invited us into his office and then he told a bouncer to go get Gorgeous. She came to the back room where we were. In the room sat me, Tony, Lamont and three of Monte's security guards. Gorgeous walks in tired, sweaty and almost nude.

"What's up?"

Lamont looks around, smiles, and then hits her across the face with the back of his hand.

"I thought I told you to make him happy," Lamont told Gorgeous. "He didn't want to Monte!" Gorgeous shouted defensively in fear. Lamont said because she had been disobedient that she had to give one of his bouncers oral sex as everyone in the room watched.

While she was doing this, Lamont took off his belt and struck her across her back like a runaway slave. Gorgeous screamed and cowered into the corner. It was a sickening sight. Here was this beautiful Amazon crying and curled up into a ball while this punk whipped and kicked her. One of the bouncers pulled her by the legs and another put his foot on her neck so Lamont could deliver good, full lashes across her butt and back. Lamont put the belt around her neck like a leash and dragged her back over to that bouncer.

"Finish!" said Lamont. While she was doing so, one of the bouncers continued to whip her across the back. By the time he came, Gorgeous was hoarse. She had temporarily lost her voice from the crying and screaming.

Lamont then made her go back out there with scars on her back and a tear stained face for the rest of the girls to see. Gorgeous sat at the bar and I went and sat next to her.

"Next time he sends me to your place, just fuck me, please," She said.

The DJ called her name for her to hit the stage. She took two shots of Jack Daniels to the head, smiled and whispered, "Gotta Go." The other girls got a chance to see her scars under the light. A dancer named Purrfect started to cry. As Gorgeous danced with an emotionless expression on her face, the other girls began to give her their tips. I put my phone number on a C-note and put it in her garter. She looked me in the eyes, but more so looking through me. "Thanks Suga." She was back in character.

I left after that. I called Aminah from Tony's house. "How's it going?" asked Aminah. I lied and told her fine. "Everyone here is fine too. Mikail, I'm glad you called because I'm moving down there in two months or so. Me and the baby are going to live with Chris. He says he has a job for me."

"A job?"

"Yes, a job. I'm just letting you know."

The conversation I had to keep short. I was happy that my son was coming.

Tony waited until I got off the phone then

shouted "Goddamn, Gorgeous can suck a golf ball through a straw!"

"Didn't that whole scene make you sick?"

"Hell naw. Fuck that bitch."

I let it go at that.

The next night I went back to the club. I decided to try my luck. I walked through without paying and one of the bouncers yelled, "Yo!" He grabbed me by the jacket and pulled me out. I grabbed him back and we tussled a little. That's when Monte said, "Hey, he's an old friend of mine. He never has to pay."

I timed it perfectly so this happened while Gorgeous was at the bar. I wanted her to see and hear it. It caught her attention. I waited until it was her turn to dance then I walked up and tipped her fifty bucks. When Gorgeous got off stage she went to the bar. She ordered her usual shots of Jack Daniels. I came over and sat next to her. "Hey Mick, I." I cut her off to properly pronounce my name for her. "Mikail." She giggled and replied "Whatever."

Lamont walked up. "Getting to know my three-hundred-dollar whore?" He was always an insecure asshole. He said it so everyone heard it. Gorgeous was so embarrassed. But humiliating Gorgeous was as pointless as beating a dead horse. She would never make eye contact with Lamont and when she looked me in the eyes she lowered her head after a second or two, almost apologetic.

I hated Lamont now and I had never respected him. I told him, "You're interrupting us." Gorgeous shook her head and tried to walk away, but I guided her back on to the barstool. I stood in front of him with my hands in my pockets and my chest out. Here I was facing off with a high roller in his own club, alone. Tony walked up on me and said, "Let's go". I gave him a look and he backed up.

Even though I was broke now, the last time anybody saw me in the city I was working up under Momo. I was connected when the set was strong. Lamont's bouncers had crowded around me so then he got balls. "Look Cuz." I cut him off. "Nigga, fuck you." The whole bar was now looking and the music had stopped.

He walked off smiling and mumbled, "Broke ass nigga." I retorted "Mama's boy" and he went into the back. I knew now that I had to leave. I knew what the wedding band on his index finger meant. I also knew that I didn't have one.

Gorgeous was in shock and so were the other girls. But if I knew Lamont, he was going to try to get me back for that. I looked at Gorgeous and ordered her like a Marine General.
"Write down your phone number." She wrote it down and then I left.

When I got back to Tony's he was all excited. "Nigga, you the man. You are the mutha fucking man." Tony was apparently unaware of the repercussions of such an action as the one I had just taken. War was declared tonight and I didn't have an army. I didn't even own a gun anymore.

Tony shouted "It looked like a stand-off at the O.K. Corral." I let him go on and on until he worked himself into a frenzy and tired himself out.

Then I asked him what had happened on the street after Momo was killed.

"It was weird. After Momo was killed and y'all left, shit just kinda cooled out." Tony then added, "Everybody thought Momo and Jamal had beef, but there was no beef. Momo and Jamal started Al-Ossrah together. Black Mafia Hustlers is just a bunch of cowboys who take turns setting each other up. They let anybody join who can turn a buck. Remember how when the set use to walk into a restaurant or bakery and the people looked up to them?"

"Yea, I remember, those were gangsters. Tony, shit just don't add up. Momo was killed in his own bed?"

"Yep." I asked if one soldier was killed in the garage and if one was killed in the house like the paper said. "Right again."

"Where was Sasquatch?"

"Probably shooting Momo." Then we both got quiet.

The next day I went to Watts to the Diamond Pawn Shop owned by Ben Diamond. He was still there, still behind the counter.

"How's the kids?"

"What kids?" I replied.

"My little Meenah and Teemah." referring to Aminah and Fatimah. I told him that they were doing fine. "I hope you're being a good husband." I didn't have the heart to tell him how Aminah and I had drifted apart. "How's Fatimah?" I answered that she too was doing fine. I told him that she was married and very happy. "That's not surprising". I asked him what he meant by that. "Everybody always thought Fatimah was weak. Fatimah was always the stronger willed and more disciplined of the two. Aminah was always a bit wild, so I know your hands are full." Then Ben asked me what I needed.

I told him that I was in trouble and that I needed a gun. He took me in the back and showed me some guns. I took the pump shotgun for the home and two pistols to carry.

A Smith and Wesson .357 and a Taurus .38 snub nose. He suggested the Glock 9mm, but I told him that I only use revolvers, automatics jam. I don't trust them.

I told Ben that I would pay him back. He said since the guns would be used to protect the Salaam girls they were a gift. I loaded the guns into the back of Tony's pick-up truck and walked back in the pawn shop where Ben and I continued to talk about Momo. Then I flat out asked him if he thought Sasquatch had killed him. He told me a story that summed up Ali's A.K.A. Sasquatch's loyalty.

"Twenty years ago when Muhammad was in his prime, he was arrested right out here in the Nickerson Garden Projects. It was sloppy. The police beat Salaam unmercifully in front of an angry crowd. Sasquatch followed the police car and while the car was stopped at a light, Sasquatch supposedly shot both policemen and blew open the door and snatched Salaam out. This probably saved Muhammad's life.

There was no real investigation. Those cops were extorting money from pimps and dealers, so when they turned up dead, the community saw nothing, and said nothing. That was Ali. He was only around 18 at the time." I thanked him and left.

Now armed, I felt a little safer. I'm sure Mustafa knew I was on the street but I guess he didn't care. I'm sure Lamont had told him, but I assumed Mustafa had forgotten or simply had bigger fish to fry. No one seemed to be concerned with the truth surrounding Momo's assassination.

Coming back from five years in Fremont I had to pick up where I last stopped. It's like I had been frozen for five years while the rest of the city continued to live and grow. Between tipping Gorgeous, sending Aminah child support and just plain living expenses, I was now down to two hundred dollars. I could tell that Ben wanted to tell me something else, but I had to put Momo in the back of my mind. I needed money, a job, a score…something.

Later that night I was at the studio with Tony. He was working on some tracks for some underground CD's. Gorgeous was there with him adding background vocals. She was extremely talented. Aperently they had hooked up at Monte's.

"What's up Mika, Mick, whatever your name is."

"Later."

I waved at her and told her that I'll be at home. By home I meant Tony's place. Gorgeous came by with Tony half past midnight. Tony left. He was on his way to Monte Carlo's.

"Gorgeous, aren't you going too?"

"No. I only work there when I'm real broke. I hate it there. I mean, the money is good. It's just that he picks on me constantly."

It was hard to listen to her while looking at her 6-foot hour glass flawless figure. I grabbed her around the waist and pulled her into Tony's room. She offered no resistance. I made love to her while she fucked me. She had the kind of personality that made me want to protect her. We laid there in Tony's bed and talked for hours about everything.

She had her head on my chest and her legs hung out of the bed. Gorgeous was the best sexual experience I had ever had.

"Mickey, will you be my man? I mean cause everybody is scared of Monte and he's scared of you." At the time when she asked me I had no idea what she was really talking about.

"I have a wife that I'm trying to reconcile with. She'll be here next week and we have a son."

"Nigga, that ain't what I mean. I need to make some money. Since I haven't been at the club, I've been dating again."

At that point her pager went off. She called him back. It was a trick. "Hey suga, ..tomorrow night, cool,, o.k.…see you then." Gorgeous then turned to me and asked me to come with her on her dates to make sure everything's okay. I told her that I didn't have time for that bullshit. I got scores to pull down.

Every night after that Gorgeous would call and we would talk. We talked about our childhood, upbringing, family, goals, dreams, everything.

We would go bowling, to the gym or to the beach and she would pay for everything. She loved soul food and New England clam chowder. She loved to read and write as much as I did. We had become friends.

Aminah and our son Hussain had come to town and they were staying with her cousin Chris. She called when Gorgeous was over and Gorgeous had answered the phone.

"Mickey, telephone!" she screamed.

"Hello, who the hell was that?" asked Aminah. "What did she call you? Did she call you Mickey? What's going on over there? I don't want Hussain hanging around no low class, low life bitches. Are you fucking that bitch? I'm on my way over."

When Aminah got there with Hussain and Chris, she came in cursing as usual.

"I'm beating that bitch's ass."

Gorgeous emerged from the bedroom and Aminah stopped in her tracks and just stared at her. She immediately felt threatened by the visually stunning presence of Gorgeous.

"You fucked her Mikail. I know you did."

During this ordeal Gorgeous remained silent. She was used to women feeling threatened by her. Aminah finally calmed down and asked me for child support.

"I need some money," said Aminah with her pouty mouth and tear stained face. I had 60 bucks to my name. Before I could open my mouth Gorgeous said "Mickey you left your money in the bedroom. I'll get it."

Gorgeous came back with 400 dollars of her own money and gave it to me. I gave the entire 400 to Aminah. Gorgeous knew that I didn't have any money. Aminah pulled me to the side and whispered,

"What's with this Mickey shit?"

"She can't pronounce my name" I told Aminah. Aminah, Hussain and Chris then left.

"You have a cute son."

"Thanks."

Gorgeous said that Hussain looked just like his momma. "I gotta go" said Gorgeous.

"Where are you going?" I asked like some sort of jealous boyfriend.

"I'm going to Monte Carlos", said Gorgeous in a pessimistic apologetic way.

"Do you know why Lamont picks on you?"

"No, why?"

"Because he's actually jealous of the attention you command. When we were kids Lamont was a momma's boy who felt insecure about his height. He was always quick to fight, always trying to prove himself to O.G.'s. Lamont feels threatened by your height and confidence."

Gorgeous laughed and replied that it takes all kinds to make a world. Then she left.

Little did I know tonight would be the night that changed my life for the rest of my life. Lamont had found out through the grapevine how close Gorgeous and I had gotten. About two hours after she left, I got a page with her code 220 which meant second to none. I returned her call immediately. She had paged me from a phone booth down the street from club Monte Carlo. She was crying and scared.

"Baby, come and get me. I need you."

"I'm on my way."

I called a cab since Tony was gone in his truck and picked her up. Her clothes were torn. She wouldn't say what had happened. When I tried to ask her, she just shook her head and put it on my shoulder. The cab driver asked where we were going. I answered that we were going back home. Gorgeous spoke up and said that we were going to the Marriott Hotel by the airport. I looked at the cab driver and repeated "The Marriott."

Gorgeous put two hundred dollars in my pocket and told me to go in and rent the room. She stayed in the cab and never got her change from me or the cab driver. Gorgeous paid as she went through life. She always tipped and she never stayed in one place long enough to leave a footprint.

As soon as we got to the room, Gorgeous started talking. "You said you'd be my man. You gotta protect me from him. How do you expect me to make your money if I keep getting my ass whipped?"

I was putting two and two together like a kindergartner, slow and patiently. Gorgeous wanted a pimp, not a boyfriend. I was a hustler and a gangster, but not a pimp. I had done it before but never full-fledged. I knew pimps, even had a few in my family but it wasn't my 'thang'. But the way Gorgeous said "money" with such conviction; I was willing to make it my 'thang'.

"Tony talks about you like you're some sort of God. He tells the girls at the club about the banks y'all robbed." I cut her off because I didn't want her to paint an unbelievable picture of me. I told her that it wasn't like we went into the vault.

"We would just rob the teller or two nearest the door. In and out in 30 seconds, with 4 to 15 grand."

"So nigga, that takes balls regardless. Tony said to me in private that you used to do hits when you were 14 or 15."

"Tony says a lot doesn't he?"

"Mickey, I'm a prostitute. I know everybody and everybody knows me. I fucked damn near every big baller to come through L.A. in the past ten years."

I asked her did she fuck Momo. “Lots of times. He was a nice, lonely old man who always paid me double and up front”

From that point on I never looked at Gorgeous in the same light. It was ironic that I fell in love with Aminah like a sister, but circumstances made her my wife. I fell in love with Gorgeous like a wife, but circumstances made her my sister.

Gorgeous had been a prostitute since the age of 15 and she knows nothing else but the game. She’s great at separating men from their money. If I was going to make this new business venture work, then I had to turn off my heart and turn up my mind.

I knew what she wanted. She wanted to work under my flag. And she knew what I wanted and that was to rise to power on the L.A. streets and redeem my name. Gorgeous went on to say how she had fucked a lot of famous people. From actors, boxers, dope dealers, basketball players, even a priest. I mean local politicians, judges, you name it. But most of her tricks were working men. I asked her if she knew Mustafa.

"Of course. But his dick can't get hard." I started to laugh until she told me he was in a wheelchair now. Apparently, he was shot in the back while I was away. I guess this was the reason for his seclusion.

I could hear the cash register as she talked. "I have nobody in my life. You're my only friend and I need you. We need each other, even if it's just temporary. What's last name?" she asked.

"Sharif"

"What does it mean?"

"Royalty"

"From now on your name is Mickey Royal. Every player has a game name."

We spent the night talking. I did mostly listening. She paced and talked all night. The more she talked, the more powerful I felt. She went to take a shower and prepare for bed. While she was in the shower, I called Tony.

"Nigga, why didn't you tell me Mustafa was in a wheelchair?"

"I forgot Mikail that you've been gone. But everybody knows. It's not exactly headline news."

I asked Tony to let me know if he sees or hears anything concerning Lamont that I might be interested in since he was always at the club.

Gorgeous emerged from the bathroom and I got off of the phone quickly.

“Who was that?”

“Just Tony”

I was lying on my back and Gorgeous straddled me and began to lick and suck on my neck. I have robbed banks, put in work, worked right next to Momo the boss but I have never felt more powerful than I did at that particular moment. I realized at that moment that I had a tiger by the tail. As Gorgeous began to perform oral sex on me, ideas of my new identity raced through my head 1,000 miles per second. MICKEY ROYAL, it had a cool ring to it.

Chapter Five

From A Meow, To A Roar

We went to work immediately. Gorgeous and I drove to Sunset Blvd in Tony's truck. She got out of the truck and began to work. Ten minutes later a white trick picked her up and drove up the street to a motel. Thirty minutes later he dropped her off. I sat there as trick after trick picked her up and dropped her back off.

We left Hollywood as the sun came up and went to Norma's, a twenty-four hour coffee house on Century and La Brea. People stared at us and the waiter asked me if Gorgeous was my woman. I told him no. He asked me if he could have her phone number. He was a nice square guy. Gorgeous had on her trade mark leather full-length trench coat. She was wearing panties and bra only underneath her coat. She had the belt tied so that you couldn't tell. But the waiter knew she was "dating" because of her thigh high boots.

Purrfect, a dancer at Monte Carlo's came in. She greeted Gorgeous by yelling,

"Hey Ho!"

Gorgeous waved her over to join us. "Monte asked about you" said Purrfect. Purrfect had a flat-chest with big hips and an ass you would have to stick your face in to appreciate. She stood about 5 feet 5 inches and she had just gotten off work. I sat silently as they talked.

Purrfect sat next to Gorgeous at our table. The waiter brought our order, finally. Gorgeous fed Purrfect from her plate. Gorgeous told Purrfect that she needed to be with Mickey Royal. She told Purrfect that I was the next King. Purrfect looked at me and said "Him? Yea right" in a condescending manner. Purrfect then formally introduced herself to me. The waiter's name was Dominick. "Yo Dominick! Here's my phone number" screamed Gorgeous.

"Call this number and my man will answer. Tell him you want to date me, and we'll hook up." Dominick looked puzzled as Purrfect started to really laugh. Gorgeous asked him, "Well, do you want to fuck me?" He began to shy away as the guys in the booth behind us turned around. "Bye Bye Dominick", said Gorgeous. She then turned to me and Purrfect and said, "Let's go".

Gorgeous was vicious and intimidating when she wanted to be. Purrfect stayed at Norma's after we left. When we got in the car Gorgeous put 870 dollars in my top pocket and kissed me on the cheek. On the ride back to Tony's she fell asleep.

We worked Sunset for the rest of that week. I had 3,374 dollars in seven days off of one hoe. At this point I had no desire to burglarize, kill, deal dope or work a 9 to 5. I loved my new profession. I kept my money at Tony's house in a sock on his top shelf in the kitchen behind the saltine crackers.
"Let's roll", I told Gorgeous.
"This early baby?"
It was 7:00pm, Gorgeous was waking up.

We would get in about 6:00am. I would wake up around noon, but Gorgeous usually slept ten to twelve hours.

Gorgeous got dolled up and told me that we couldn't work Hollywood tonight. She said that it's vice night on Sunset. Hooker and homeless round-up. So we hit Figueroa & 83rd St. Gorgeous really stood out among the prostitutes on Figueroa. They were mostly crack heads who would did blow jobs for $20 and sell pussy for $50. It was slow for a while until a car pulled up.

She strutted over to the car like Marilyn Monroe in her prime. She let her hands drop and leaned her perfectly chiseled body into the car. Words were exchanged, and she got into the car. They drove to a dead-end street around the corner and cut off the head lights. I always followed her dates. It was my job to protect her.

I parked where I could see, but couldn't be seen. They got out of the car and climbed into the back seat. Gorgeous began to kick the door. The trick was on top of her. I could see his head.

The car was rocking from side to side. Gorgeous was my whore second, but my friend first. We were developing a bond. I saw what appeared to be the trick's hand going up and down. I assumed he was fucking her doggy style and spanking her on her ass.

The back door opened up long enough for her to crawl halfway out. She screamed, "Mickey!" then he pulled her back into the car by his hands which were wrapped around her neck. I wasn't armed, so I reached under the seat and grabbed a crowbar. I drove up to the car, hopped out with the crowbar and burst the driver's side window.

I opened the door and pulled him out and began to beat him. He crumbled immediately. People from the neighborhood came outside and the police pulled up. Gorgeous was staggering away. She didn't even look back. She just kept walking.

I was arrested and charged with assault. The cops interrogated me all night. Not about pimping or the assault but about the murder of Momo and the disappearance of Ali a.k.a. Sasquatch.

"How much did Mustafa pay y'all?"

I didn't answer.

"Three people died, Mr. Sharif."

I still didn't say a word. Then the cop said that the guy in the house was killed with the same gun as Muhammad Salaam but that the guy in the garage was killed with a different gun. Another cop came in and whispered in his ear and the aggressive cop left.

The new cop gave me his card and told me that his name was Special Agent Murphy and if I ever felt like talking I should call him. Then Agent Murphy took me back to my cell. I didn't use my phone call. I just sat there for three days. I sat in that cell thinking about Gorgeous, but mostly what that cop was saying about Momo. Shit just didn't add up.

"Sharif! visitor!"

I went to go see who it was. It was Chris and Aminah.

"Are you O.K.?" asked Aminah. I answered that I was cool.

"Your ho came by and told me what had happened. Back in your element, right baby?"

"Don't start", I told Aminah. We argued for a minute, then the guard escorted me to Agent Murphy's office.

"Look, I don't' know shit!"

"Just sit down."

"I'd rather stand."

"Lucky break. The guy you assaulted refused to press charges after I told him that you were a hit man in the Muslim Mafia."

"There is no such thing."

"The charge is now reckless endangerment and disorderly conduct."

The next morning when I went to court, my bail was set at $10,000 only because of my record. I was in my cell for two hours before my bail was posted. I dressed out and as I walked down the hallway Gorgeous and Purrfect were standing there. Purrfect, who was more actress than dancer, was applauding. Apparently Gorgeous had paid my bail. They were both standing there looking delicious.

"About time," I said to Gorgeous as the cops looked on. Gorgeous put her arms around me and yelled "My man is free." I could tell that Gorgeous was putting on a show trying to show Purrfect that she had someone in her corner. "Goddamn Mickey Royal. Mickey muthafuckin Royal" said Purrfect.

"You the man!" Gorgeous shouted.

"Let's get the fuck out of this police station it stinks."

Gorgeous had gotten Purrfect to drive her to pick me up. She had told Purrfect about what had happened. Purrfect was excited that I actually went to jail for Gorgeous. "You fucked him up for touching your Bitch!" said Purrfect. Since Gorgeous had already seemed to have gotten Purrfect primed, I decided to spit some Game. Purrfect was only twenty-two and looked up to Gorgeous. Purrfect wasn't a prostitute, just an exotic dancer. Purrfect didn't strike me as the dependent type, but this little incident had her nose wide open. So I began talking to her. "You women have it made."

"How you figure?"

"Because you have a pussy. You're born with it. It costs you nothing to produce. You can't ever run out of it and men can't live without it." I had her undivided attention at this point so I continued. "I provide a service. This is a team, a family. And on every team each member has a specific job. Gorgeous keeps me together and I keep us moving forward."

Gorgeous told Purrfect to drop us both off at Motel 6. When Purrfect pulled off, Gorgeous went into the lobby and called a cab. "I didn't want her to know where you lived" Gorgeous told me.

On the way home, Gorgeous fell asleep. She always fell asleep on long car rides. But before she laid her head in my lap she put five-hundred and seventy-five dollars in my hand and said,

"While you were gone."

"This is it! I was gone for three days."

She looked at me in anger with a ferocious look on her face rivaling a lioness preparing for a strike against a much larger opponent. She then said "Minus a grand for your bail, remember. And I paid

Aminah your child support." Then she rolled her eyes at me and put her head in my lap and said, "Mickey, I would never steal from us."

I knew we couldn't keep operating like this. It was my nature to grow, to expand, and I kept hearing Gorgeous voice, "The Next King". It rang over and over in my ears.

The next afternoon while Gorgeous was still sleep I went to see Hussain. While I was playing with my son, I started a conversation with Chris about the streets. Over the years Chris kinda kept his distance from me.

Every time we talked he had some way of trying to fix Aminah and I back together. "She dresses like a whore. She talks like a sailor and she claims to be a Muslim woman.

She's fulla shit," I said. Then Chris replies, "Are you serious Nigga. What about you? Everybody knows the shit you got going. You live with sneaky ass Tony and a hooker."

I cut him off and I said what I do for a living and who I am are totally separate. My religion is who I am. What I do for a living is just a job. Chris then laughed sarcastically and said "Both you and Aminah are hypocrites."

I was speechless because he had me stumped with no reply. Anger and resentment came over me as I watched him play with my son on the floor.

I knew then that I was on the verge of losing my family and I wanted them back. Something had to change. Aminah walked in tired. She was working at Ralph's supermarket as a cashier. She was carrying groceries and glad to see me. She was only working part-time.

I asked her if she would prefer $125 a week or just $500 on the first of the month. Aminah told me that she would prefer $250 per week and that working doesn't agree with her. She also wanted to know when I was going to start taking care of her. I looked at Chris who was sitting on the couch and told him, "See what I mean, still spoiled, still selfish." Turning to Aminah I asked her "Why don't you ask David to take care of you." Her face filled with disappointment and shock.

She then pushed past me and went to her room. At that point I left.

I knew that I still loved Aminah, but I came to the sad realization that we would never be together again. Trust is like virginity, once lost, it can never be regained. When I saw her face, nothing but hate entered my mind. I'm smart enough to know that this relationship is a potentially dangerous situation and that it's best for all parties involved if she and I part ways.

When I came back home I found Gorgeous asleep on the couch. I had managed to sock away close to $6,000 and the month wasn't over yet. At the rate we were going, this was a bigger, steadier pay-off than working for Momo. Plus it was all mine. I answered to no one. Gorgeous was snoring hard but my anger and greed, brought on by Aminah, made me lash out at her.

"Get up!"

She got up and as she was getting dressed, she sat on the floor and started to cry. She was tired. I knew this pace couldn't continue.

"Are you okay?"

"I'm fine" she said as she wiped the tears from her face. I realized then that I couldn't have my cake and eat it too. The more I tried to get close to Aminah the further apart it pushed Gorgeous and me. I had to make a choice. Gorgeous was a giver, Aminah was a taker. The choice was clear.

We were in Tony's truck on our way to work. We pulled up on Sunset. Gorgeous and I always had a long, maybe 15 minutes or so conversation before she actually got out of the car.

"I'll be back baby," I said.

"Where? When? Mickey don't leave me." I told her that I had something to take care of. Gorgeous leaned over to kiss me on the neck and got out of the truck. She was in place one minute before she got a trick. She got in his car and they left.

I then drove over to Monte Carlo's and sat in the parking lot. I was waiting for Purrfect. When she pulled up I called her name and she came over to the truck. She got in and we started to talk. Purrfect asked where Gorgeous was. I told her that she was working.

"So...what's up?" I answered Purrfect by asking whether or not she had been thinking about what we had talked about. Purrfect told me that she had thought about it but that it wasn't for her. "Why should I give you my money? You ain't dancing. No disrespect or anything.

I would love to have you in my corner, but you don't even have a ring. What if I get with you and you go to jail. I'm left out in the cold. Mickey, I think you're good for Gorgeous, but I don't wanna dance for the rest of my life. I mean what do you really do for Gorgeous?" I realized I was losing this conversation so I gave Purrfect my pager number and Tony's home phone number then I left.

I went back to check on Gorgeous and sat in the car parked in the spot. I sat there all night. Gorgeous finally pulls up and gets out of a limousine, looks around and walks over to the car. She hands me a fist full of hundreds and hops in the back seat. "Let's go", she says. I left not knowing what the excitement was all about, or where we were going.

Gorgeous finally told me to drive to the Greyhound Bus Station to pick up her friend, Candy. "Mickey, Candy is a dancer and she has no place to stay. I talked to her on the phone in the limo. I told her what the set up was and she was with it."

"Do we have to pick her up now?"

"Hell yeah!" Gorgeous replied.

When we got to the bus station Candy was outside the gate waiting on us. She had one suitcase and a black eye.

"Is this Mickey Royal?" asked Candy.

"Yep. This is my daddy." Candy introduced herself to me as Lydia, but then added that I was to call her Candy, that she hated being called Lydia. She was about 27, but looked no more than 19. She had run away from her pimp only after a week of moving back in with him.

The black eye had come from her baby's father, who put her out two weeks prior. I could tell Candy was wild. "You got some blow?" Before I could answer Gorgeous told her that she had been clean for three years.

I took Candy to the Sheraton Hotel and paid two weeks in advance. I didn't want to and really couldn't afford it but Gorgeous reassured me that Candy was a pro and that it was an investment. We walked Candy to her room and got her settled in. I left and waited for Gorgeous downstairs in the car. Ten minutes later Gorgeous gets in the car.

"It's on now, Candy is good to go."

"Where do you know Candy from?"

Gorgeous told me that she had been engaged to Candy's brother at one time and that she and Candy's brother had met while in the Marines together. "You were in the marines?" Gorgeous answered with peacock-ish pride in her voice, "Nigga, I was in Desert Storm." I was shocked, amazed a little and even impressed.

As we rode, we talked. She did all of the talking, I did all of the listening. I found out that Gorgeous had been in combat in Iraq and Kuwait. I had to ask her.

"What happened? How did you end up a..?"

"A what?" she screamed. She filled with anger and rolled down the window. The cold air forced trapped tears from their ducts down to her cheeks.

Gorgeous was a teen prostitute. Then when she cleaned up her act she enlisted in the Marine Corps. She went on to tell me that after she got out of the service, she couldn't find a job so she went back to the streets. Gorgeous had gotten a dishonorable discharge. She never explained why. Prostitute was not a job description for Gorgeous, it was an identity. Gorgeous had long since made peace with who she was.

When we got in, I counted the take. The fist full of hundreds Gorgeous had given me was twelve hundred dollars plus $179 she had made before the limo came. "How did you make so much so soon?" I had to wake her up to ask her.

"This Asian guy with a foreign accent offered me $100 for straight sex. I told him to make it $200. When we got to his mansion he offered me $600 instead to give me a facial golden shower.

Then he gives me $600 more to let his 15-year-old nephew have anal sex with me. Tomorrow night he's supposed to pick me up again. He said that he'll have a grand for ten minutes worth of work."

Her eyes awaited my approval before she went back to sleep. I granted my reluctant okay. I never asked details about her dates again. Gorgeous, I considered her a friend. Where I went, she went. I hated the fact that she was being degraded this way for me. But Gorgeous wasn't stupid, nor was she a victim. She knew if I became King, I would need a Queen. She felt I had the credentials and she was putting her bid in early.

Maybe she cared about me or maybe it was all business. Who knows? Who cares? All I knew was she trusted and believed in what I was doing to the point where she jumped in with both feet and never looked back.... That's dedication.

With two hoes now, the stash was growing. In the first seven days with Candy and Gorgeous I made $6,730. I took that money and bought a 1970 black Coup-De-Ville Cadillac convertible.

Hollywood was hot and now with two fine whores who worked together and looked after one another, I had a little more free time.

I dropped the girls off on Hollywood Blvd near Vine St. Tony and I went to a strip club with his girlfriend Teresa and her cousin, Nikki. Nikki resembled Vanessa Williams, but she was only 21 years old. She was about 5'7" and thin. She was half White and half Mexican.

Nikki had thick blonde hair, green eyes and a wide smile full of bright white teeth. She was fine, all face but skinny. She worked at the Fox Hills Mall at the Hot Dog on a Stick.

We arrived at the club.

"Oh..my…God, Teresa. This is a Go-Go club" said Nikki. "Tony why are we here?" Tony leaned back and said, "Y'all wait here in the car. I got to run in and get something." I had realized just then we were at the Monte Carlo. I sat in the car and talked to Nikki. Nikki and Teresa were singers who Tony was trying to sign to his management company, then to get them a record deal.

Tony came out a few minutes later with some weed. Neither he nor I smoked, but Teresa did heavily. Nikki decided to smoke, but just for a minute and to fit in.

"You belong in diamonds," I told Nikki.

"I know. I just wish these men out here felt that way," agreed Nikki. Teresa gave her a high five in support. We drove to the pier in Santa Monica for a seafood dinner. "Lobsters all around", I announced to the waiter.

"Watch out now cause I ain't washing no dishes" Nikki told me.

"Naw Baby. I got it under control."

"Is that right?" Nikki said.

"Oh absolutely!"

Our tennis match flirting continued until the food arrived. While Nikki and I flirted, Teresa and Tony kissed and giggled. We all acted like junior high school students that night. We enjoyed the lobsters and I enjoyed the big shot pit stop so to speak. I hadn't actually been on a date in years. I felt good. I was big daddy and myself and relaxed all at the same time.

Nikki and I really hit if off. After dinner, all four of us walked on the beach. The echoes of the waves crashing against the rocks combined with a light wind added to the angelic state of the evening. Just as the waves crashed against the rocks, reality crashed into my fantasy as my pager went off and I looked down to see an unfamiliar number with 220 behind it.

"I need to find a phone." Nikki reached into her purse and pulled out her cell phone.

"Come pick us up. We're in Malibu"

"I'm on my way." Gorgeous then gave me the address. "Who was that? Yo baby momma or something?" Nikki asked. I ignored her and motioned for Tony to come here.

"We gotta pick up my girls in Malibu."

"Now?"

"Yep, right now."

Nikki and Teresa had no idea where we were going. But they complained the whole trip. We finally got there. I ran in to find Gorgeous on some

man's lap and Candy standing by the door.
"We're ready." Candy said to me. I didn't acknowledge her nor did I even make eye contact. I looked at Gorgeous and asked,
"We ready?"
"I gotta go. My ride is here." Gorgeous said to the old fat rich trick.
"Where can I reach you?" Gorgeous looked at me for approval and I nodded my head in agreement. She told the man Tony's phone number and we left.

"How are we going to all fit back here?" said Candy. I again ignored her and Gorgeous answered, "We'll fit." Gorgeous got in first and then Candy sat on her lap. Candy started licking Nikki's leg. She didn't know Nikki but Candy was high and didn't give a fuck. Nikki told her, "Don't start what you can't finish."

Candy was coked up and her inhibitions disappeared when she was high. Nikki and Teresa got to smoking weed and laughing and daring each other all the way back to the Sheraton. When Candy got out, Nikki got out with her. I dropped Teresa and Tony back off at Tony's place.

We let them go in and have some privacy, then Gorgeous and I got a room at the Motel 6.

"It was slow tonight daddy" said Gorgeous, as she handed me $650.

"Is this from you or Candy?"

"Both."

Gorgeous went on to say, "I told you Candy was a pro. We used to work Oakland and Vegas together. In less than a week that light-skinned bitch will be down with us. Watch, Candy's about to wrap Nikki's stuck up ass the fuck up and turn her out."

Gorgeous was proud that her home girl had the Midas touch. She also spoke now with a sense of power because some of my game had come through her. We laid there in bed together looking up at the ceiling discussing future plans.

Sure enough, Gorgeous was right. Tony paged me the next morning.

"Nigga, guess what?"

"What man?" I asked pretending to be uninterested.

"Nikki quit her job and told Teresa she is going to be a thousand-dollar call girl and from what I understand, Candy and Nikki have been selling pussy all night in the bar near the Sheraton to tricks in the hotel, even the manager."

I told Gorgeous and she was furious. She didn't respond the way I expected.

"That slick bitch!"

"What?"

"Mickey roll to the Sheraton now!" As soon as we got to Candy's room Gorgeous started in on her.

"I need the take." Gorgeous said to Candy. Candy reluctantly handed her $600.

"Nikki go wait in the car. We're parked right by the exit", said Gorgeous as she handed Nikki the keys.

Gorgeous waited until Nikki was in the elevator going down. I stood over by the door, posing, pretending that I knew what was going on. Gorgeous started going through Candy's drawers. Candy was pulling on her, but Gorgeous is twice her size. She just tossed Candy on the bed like a child. Gorgeous handed me a paper sack full of cash, mostly small bills.

“See Mickey, this bitch’s been dating on your money in this room and holding out. Dancing, parties, what else? Don’t lie bitch. I know you.”

“Come on girl.” Candy pleaded.

“Fuck that!”

Then Gorgeous punched her oldest friend in the jaw. Gorgeous started to kick her in the stomach. She grabbed Candy and shoved her face down into the pillow to drown out the screams.

Gorgeous held Candy’s face down with one hand and beat Candy with her shoe on the butt and back. “I’m sorry, please, that’s my sore!” I counted about $1,800 in the bag. When Gorgeous and I walked out, we were met by a trick in the hall.

“Is Candy in?”

“Why?” said Gorgeous.

“It’s personal.”

“She’s sick, but I’m available.”

The trick handed Gorgeous $150 and asked could he watch while she ate his wife’s pussy.

Gorgeous looked at me as she handed me the 150 dollars and said, "I'll be down in 30 minutes." Gorgeous then walked into his room.

When I got to the car Nikki asked;

"Where's Candy?"

"She's working, like you need to be doing."

"I don't mind like actors and athletes, but I ain't with that standing on the corner stuff."

"What has Candy told you?"

"She said that it's organized and you're real cool and they don't stand on corners and you buy your employees cars and shit."

Nikki went on and on about this and that but it was mostly lies. I liked the sound of what she was saying though. I saw the potential, but you do have to spend money to make money. I had some ideas I wanted to try. The pimp game is about to meet a gangster.

Nikki had an innocent look about her just like Purrfect, even though they looked totally different. Purrfect was dark-skinned with a perfect body and very voluptuous. Nikki was white looking and skinny with green eyes. She looked exotic. Cleopatra came to mind.

"It's exotic" Nikki A.K.A. Cleo said. Her attitude was that of a bored teenager who was anxious to try the new designer drug at a club. Gorgeous got in the car and said,

"Hey Kitty because you have cat eyes."

"It's Cleopatra"

Gorgeous turned and smiled at me in victory.

"Where do you live?" I asked Cleo.

"I share an apartment with Teresa in Hawthorne."

I drove her home and we exchanged phone numbers. "We'll be in touch" I said, then drove off. Sometimes I wondered in detail exactly what Gorgeous did with her tricks but I never asked again after the other night. I guess because I wanted to know, but then again, I didn't.

"I don't want you to work this week", I told Gorgeous.

"Okay…but why?"

"Because I want you to hang with Cleo all week.

Go shopping."

"Gotcha", she replied.

I gave her $1,000 of the $1,800 I got from Candy and told her to spend every cent on Cleo. Gorgeous remained silent. "I got some footwork to do." I told her. I drove to the airport and rented a black Corvette for a week and dropped Gorgeous off with the Vette.

"I'll see you in a week."

"Okay, page me.", Gorgeous replied.

I had been formulating a plan in my head for a while. Now it was time to put this plan into motion. Every man or woman plays the best hand with the cards they're dealt. It was now my turn to deal.

Chapter Six

The Royal Family

I had quite a stash put away. Gorgeous had Nikki and Candy under her spell and she was under mine. Candy would work near the Hollywood and Vine area. Gorgeous would work Sunset and Nikki was on Figueroa.

Since Nikki was White, I put her on all black Figueroa and she stuck out like a sore thumb. The experiment worked. Nikki made over $700 a night, average. I was now making a minimum of 2 grand a day easy. We would work seven days a week.

I got a call from Nikki one night. I called her back on her cell phone.

"Mickey?"

"What?" I answered.

"Some nigga over here is talking bout this corner is his. He said every he on Figueroa between 40th and 85th Street has to pay. He told me to move my ass up, around 104th Street or break bread."

"So what did you do?"

"I stayed where you dropped me off, then he left. He came back an hour later, punched me in the stomach and took my money."

"Where are you now?"

"The taco stand"

"I'm on my way."

Nikki wasn't a pro. Gorgeous knew exactly what to do in situations like these but I knew extortion well. I went and picked up Candy and Gorgeous and drove straight to Nikki. She got in the car. We drove around looking for this pimp who broke Nikki. We were unsuccessful in our attempt to locate this mystery pimp.

"I'm hungry", moaned Candy. I looked at her with frustration and disappointment until Gorgeous replied, "Me too." We drove to Norma's and got a table for four.

"Mr. Royal," said Nikki.

"What?"

"That's him!" said Nikki pointing to this nigga through the glass window. I recognized him as Jackie A.K.A. Jack Frost (they called him Jack Frost cause he was cold on his hoes).

I told Gorgeous to pay for the meals and to bring the car around to the front and to leave it running. Gorgeous did so without hesitation. Candy went with Gorgeous and Nikki came with me. I walked up to Jack Frost in a confrontational manner.

"Hey Blood!" He recognized Nikki and said, "I thought she was an outlaw, but you know the game, little man." Jackie stood about 6'6" and was old enough to be my father maybe even grandfather.

When Gorgeous pulled up, I hit Jackie in the stomach then a right and left hook to the jaw. The punches staggered him. He hit the ground. I went through his pockets retrieving my money and whatever he had. As I turned to get into the car he pulled out a pistol while my back was turned. Nikki screamed "Look out!" As I turned around Jack shot me in the upper right portion of my chest. As he got up to run I heard two shots. Jack fell forward, then back, then finally ending up in a fetal position. Gorgeous had started carrying a pistol since she was attacked that night. A .22 caliber two shot Derringer. She hit Jackie in the butt with one shot and in the back of the knee with the other.

She being a vet she could have killed him if she wanted. But killing him wasn't her mission, helping me was. Without missing a beat, Gorgeous placed a hysterical Nikki in the car. Gorgeous dropped Candy and Nikki off at Teresa's apartment after dropping me off at Daniel Freeman Hospital. She pulled in doing about 50 miles an hour. She almost hit an ambulance.

I was immediately snatched out of the car and placed on a gurney. I was rushed through these double doors. I was going in and out of consciousness. The last word I remember hearing was Demerol. I awoke in my room to find Gorgeous sitting there crying. She was so excited to see I was still alive. I was the one shot but there I was consoling her. She had her head on the side of my bed as I just stroked her hair telling her everything's gonna be okay.

Then in walks Agent Murphy. "Having a bad day? He asked. I had no words for him. Gorgeous asked me if I wanted anything from the vending machine, then she excused herself. Agent Murphy kept asking me questions about Ali, Mustafa and what Momo and I used to discuss if anything. It was easy to tune him out with all of the Demerol they had given me.

Agent Murphy handed me his card yet again and left as the doctor came in. I was told I was being discharged and free to go. Gorgeous walks back in behind the doctor just as Murphy leaves. Gorgeous had been in my room all night. As soon as we got in the car my thoughts shifted back to business.

"I can't watch all of you at once. I'm gonna have to consolidate the Family," I said to Gorgeous as we exited the hospital parking lot.

I was still bandaged and quite sore. Gorgeous was conservative in the way she dressed when she wasn't working. If she wasn't hooking, she didn't look like a hooker. Well, except for her four inch clear heals. It was time to expand and Gorgeous and I knew it.

I had nearly 25 grand in cash at Tony's place. I gave him two grand and Gorgeous and I packed up and moved out. It was time to organize. First, I incorporated Royal Family Entertainment. I got each girl her own business card with lingerie photos on the card. The top of the card read Royal Family Entertainment with the girl's picture on it, her name below the picture and the card also had the house phone number on it. When we took the pictures, the girls assumed they were for a scrap book for sentimental reasons.

I leased two cars, one for myself and one for Gorgeous. I leased a Lincoln Town Car for me and a Lincoln Navigator for Gorgeous. I also rented a four-bedroom house over on Jefferson, near

Arlington in the Historic West Adams district.

For a week I let the girls take off while I soul searched and organized an effective plan where the girls would work less and make more in a protected and in a safe environment. All week Candy, Nikki and Gorgeous were going to Disneyland, the beach, riding around in Gorgeous' Navigator, shopping and shit, a regular vacation. I was incognito the entire week formulating an effective plan.

I took the liberty of making up all four rooms as mini suites. Each room had a full-sized bed, dresser, vanity mirror and a small sitting area. Each room had a different theme. I leased two more cars. A Lexus GS400 and a convertible Corvette. All of the cars were candy apple red with white interior.

My Town Car's plate read M. Royal. Gorgeous' Navigator's plate read Royal 1. The Lexus GS400's plate read Royal 2 and Corvette's read Royal 3. I was paying $2,500 a month in cars alone. $2,000 a month to rent the house, but I figured it would pay off.

I bought them all cell phones. I called Gorgeous on hers.

"Gorgeous, bring the family home."

"Mickey, we're at Magic Mountain."

"Look woman. Enjoy yourselves and have everybody at the house between 11:00pm and midnight." I demanded in a joking way.

"We'll be there at 11:00pm sharp, Baby."

That new Navigator had taken a lot of stress off of Gorgeous, as well as off of the ladies. They were starting to see a return on their investment. Where traditional pimps kept all, I had come up with a plan to keep less and yet, have more at the same time make and keep my ladies rich and happy. It was important to me to see them as successful as I was becoming. They were gonna be a reflection of me. Their success was my success.

Gorgeous was true to her word. 11:00pm sharp she pulls up with Candy and Nikki. We sat at the dining table together like the Family we were. I sat at the head for obvious reasons and began.

"Here are your business cards. There will be no more selling pussy on street corners. Each of you has a room as well as a car. All business is done here. By your bedside table is a doorbell buzzer. When you push it, the light outside of your door turns red. This lets me know if there's any danger. Also, pussy is not sold everyday by everyone. You will have a schedule.

As I was giving this speech I looked at their faces and all were mesmerized, so I continued. "The money will all come to me. I'll take 40% and your 60% will be in check form from Royal Family Entertainment. You'll file taxes as an entertainer, a private dancer. This way you'll build your credit. Every girl you bring in, you'll get 10% of her gross. It will show up on your checks. This will give you more of an incentive to work harder and expand the family quickly.

Like I said, these rooms are yours only. You can live here and work here, or just work here. Here are contracts and the contracts state that if you leave Royal Family Entertainment before the end of your contract then you will be billed for the cars and rent. If you fulfill your contract, just two years, the car is yours. The schedule is from 12:00pm to 8:00pm, sex is sold. 9:00pm to 2am you'll dance at a strip club. From 2:30am to 6:00am you'll work either the after-hour joints or the card casinos. The shifts are rotated and one girl is always off on each particular shift." I also informed them that I would live in the house from time to time.

"Can we dance anywhere we want? I mean, does it have to be Monte Carlos?" Gorgeous asked in a fearful concerned tone. "I want you to stay there. I have my reasons." The truth was I wanted spies and eyes on Monte since he was so close to Mustafa now.

The ladies were ecstatic about the new organization. Even Candy could see we were on the verge of something big. Also, to keep women like Nikki, changes had to be made. I went on to say, "New or first-time tricks you take to the motel. No first timers at the house. After turning that trick, you hand him your card. From then on out, you can date him here."

This will lessen the possibility of physical danger, jail, trouble etc. "Besides, we're family and families look out for each other," said Cleopatra. "Yea, we're Royal's Family... No, The Royal Family." said Candy. I continued. "Everyone has a phone in her room. Look, go to work and keep the house filled."

"Okay daddy," Gorgeous replied.

Immediately this idea took off. There was something about our professional set up that made it possible for the ladies to charge more and attract a better class of trick. The next night Gorgeous brought in $700 from just three tricks. 1:30pm, 3:30pm and4:15pm. Then she walked around in lingerie and watched television.

Cleopatra had five tricks at $1,800 total and Candy had two at $200 total. It wasn't even 6:00pm yet and $2,900 had been generated. They were still on the clock until 8:00pm. Tricks were willing to pay more in a safe, comfortable environment. We had gone past just pimping and hoeing. This was now an escort service/brothel.

Then the phone rang. Cleopatra answered "Royal Family Entertainment, how may I help you?"

"Oh, I was calling to speak with Candy. We had a date tonight."

"Candy's busy right now. Perhaps you'd be interested in dating me."

After she described herself, the caller was on his way. By the time he got to the door Candy was finished with her 5:00pm appointment.

"Hey, Baby," said Candy to the 6:00pm appointment as the 5:00pm appointment kissed her on the neck and left. But the 6:00pm had changed his mind and he now wanted Cleo. Cleo took him to her room and turned him in 15 minutes for $175. Candy was furious. Here it was our grand opening and Candy blew her top.

"Mickey, tell that yella bitch if she steals another client of mine she's gonna get her ass beat!"

"I ain't telling her shit. Next time handle your business!" Candy went back to her room...mad.

The girls then started getting ready to go to the clubs.

A club called Mae Westside in Hollywood. The dancing gives them a chance to get more customers. Now with cars, I don't have to pick them up, but I still keep watch. Cleopatra came out first. I told her to stay together with all of the family. So Gorgeous, Candy and Cleopatra piled up in Gorgeous' Navigator and went to work.

About an hour later the phone rang.

"Royal Family Entertainment," I said. It was Tony.

"What up"

"Purrfect just called over here looking for Gorgeous. She's in jail."

"Who's in jail, nigga?"

"Purrfect,"

The next day Gorgeous and I, went to visit her. Purrfect had 14 days left on a 30-day sentence on some credit card scam bullshit she and another dancer from Monte Carlo's were doing. Jail had not broken her. She walked up to the glass with her head held high, making eye contact with everyone.

Purrfect picked up the phone.

"Hey girl" said Purrfect.

"What was the emergency?" asked Gorgeous.

"I gotta get outta here. Did you see that guard that brought me in?"

"Yea"

"Every night he comes into my cell and rapes my cellmate Fantasy and today he said that tomorrow would be my turn. I'm scared girl."

"If you were with Mickey, he'd take care of that". They went on to talk without me in the conversation. I walked away from the glass and went over to the vending machine and got some orange juice. When we got into the car Gorgeous gave me my assignment or proposition, if you will. "If you keep Purrfect from getting raped, she'll join the family."

That night I called Chris and explained the job to him and he agreed. I picked Chris up and we drove to the jail and waited in the car at the employee exit. Purrfect told Gorgeous that his name was Leon Parks and he drove a 1991 Thunderbird.

We sat and sat.

"How's Aminah?" I asked making small talk.

"You'd know muthafucka if you came by."

Chris was always the leader when we were growing up because he was Momo's nephew. But Momo was dead, Chris is broke, but judging by the way he's talking to me I feel no one had told him. Before I could put Chris in his place, out drove Leon. "That's him," I said. As I started the car we began to follow him. All while we followed Leon I started to feel 17 years old again. Chris was steady shouting orders, "Turn left! Slow down!" That nigga was getting on my nerves.

Chris was the boss over me, Tony and Lamont but that was a long ass time ago. Now all three of us were doing better than him but Chris still had the air of an inheritor. Aminah had already adjusted from princess to pauper in Fremont.

We pulled up right behind Leon in his driveway. I reminded Chris not to kill him, just scare him a little. "Can I help you brothers?" asked Leon. Chris grabbed him as I put a .357 Magnum to his head and we put him in the trunk. Chris was excited. It was just like the old days. We drove to Compton, over behind the construction where Skateland skating rink was being torn down on Central Ave. When I opened the trunk, Leon was petrified. Chris grabbed him by the throat and pulled him out of the car and began to pistol whip him while I talked.

"A Brotha, some of those women on C-Block have brothers, uncles, fathers, husbands and friends like me. If I hear of one more case of abuse of any kind by anyone, I'm gonna slit your mother's throat in front of you before I slit yours. Do I make myself clear? Oh, and by the way, my name is Mickey Royal and I know where you live." I said this to Leon making eye contact the entire time. "I took his ID with me. I have friends at the DMV. I have friends at Equifax. There's nowhere you can go that I can't find you."

After he crapped his pants we made him strip totally naked then we threw him back in the trunk and dropped him back off on his front door step. That little run brought back a lot of memories. I paid Chris $1,000 bucks and decided to use him in the future. These new cats can't handle themselves like Chris can.

The next night Gorgeous got a call from Purrfect. Apparently Purrfect had been bragging about her so-called people who were going to take care of Leon. 24 hours later Leon is back at work with a new attitude and new scars all over his face. Gorgeous was telling me how excited Purrfect was to have such people in her corner and how powerful she felt.

Two weeks later Gorgeous, Candy, Cleo and I picked up Purrfect and her cellmate named Fantasy who was equally impressed at how Leon was nullified. Just like a young man who joins a gang or an old man who joins a lodge, the throw-a-ways, like me, just wanted a place to belong.

Fantasy was a timid, kinda spacey woman with slow speech. But she resembled Lisa Bonet and Arnelle Simpson. She was fine, but a bit of a push over. We all rode in Gorgeous' Navigator to the house which the girls called The Royal Palace. I took Purrfect and Fantasy to the side and explained the operation.

"Look Purrfect. Let Fantasy stay at your place until I rent another house."

"Okay Mickey. Whatever you say" said Purrfect.

I rented a three-bedroom house for Purrfect and Fantasy. They went to work immediately. Purrfect was smart and hardworking. She set up a computer system and went on-line for more tricks. She would rent a limo (with her own money) and pick up rich tricks on business trips at the airport.

With Purrfect's new system she and Fantasy were grossing 25% more than Gorgeous, Candy and Cleopatra. On the average, Royal Palace No. 1 grossed $1,500-2,000 a day and Royal Palace No.2 pulled in $1,900-3,000 daily. Which made my cut $800 from Palace No.1 and $1200 from Palace No.2 give or take on average.

In Fantasy's first week she grossed $5,700 alone, of course with the help of Purrfect's system. I collected all $5,700 from Fantasy and the following week she received a check for $3,420.

Gorgeous insisted on keeping none of her money. She kicked in every dime she made. I never cut her a check. I didn't even know her real name.

Purrfect introduced me to a new girl named Baby Girl. Baby Girl was short and barely 18 years old. I still to this day have no idea where they met. Baby Girl stood about 5 feet, 1 inch with a 38 double D cup bra size. She was built for sex. She had an ass like a horse and a concave stomach.

She was too young to know her true value. Purrfect charged an L.A. Laker $500 to fuck Baby Girl. She told him that Baby Girl was only 16 and still in high school. With Baby Girl at Palace No. 2 the take nearly doubled.

Unionized prostitution brought out a better class of trick. Sometimes it's not what you do so much as how you do it. We were making so much money I even hired a retired L.A.P.D. officer from the Rampart division named Cliff, to watch house No. 2 from 1:00pm to 8:00pm. I paid him 1,000 a week cash to sit in the living room and watch TV, plus all the free young pussy he could handle, which wasn't much at his age.

Customers would call the number on the card. The phone rang at both houses and now only Purrfect or Gorgeous would answer the phones. The trick would ask to speak with say, Cleopatra.

Gorgeous or Purrfect would make an appointment for her. When the trick arrived, Cleo would have to point him out to make sure he wasn't a first timer. Then she could take him to her room.

He pays Cleo only once they're in her room. After the trick has been turned, Cleo then takes the money to Gorgeous or myself to be recorded and filed. It wasn't long before my system hit the streets. It pissed off Gorilla pimps who started losing their hoes left and right.

Every where I went, hoes would approach me to work for me or to set up a Palace in their apartment complex. Gangsters were calling me the Meyer Lansky of The Pimp Game. Pimps like Jake Frost were becoming obsolete. The man who refuses to grow, grows smaller.

Nevertheless, the cash kept coming in.

We, the family, all went to Tony's shop one day together. I walked in with Candy, Baby Girl, Gorgeous, Fantasy, Purrfect and Cleopatra. I was looking and feeling like a king.

"Tony!" I shouted.

"What's up nigga?"

"From now on The Royal Family only gets their hair done here." Tony nodded in agreement with a Kool-Aid smile across his face. I was the only pimp who had women who drove Mercedes and Corvettes.

One night everyone had the night off. Candy, Cleo, Gorgeous and I sat at the table. Cleo, who was an incredible cook, prepared an unbelievable feast. We sat and ate as a family. Then what happened next I'll never forget. Cleopatra just started in. "My family would get together like this every Sunday, but it was so phony.

I remember when I told my father that I was moving out of Teresa's apartment to become a call girl. His reply was, be careful. Teresa said that they haven't called or anything." Then she looked around the table with tears in her eyes and said, "You guys are the only real family I have."

We were quiet as Cleo continued, "I never got any attention growing up." Candy cut her off and said, "All of that is over now. You're Royalty." "I got plenty of attention growing up," Gorgeous said as she excused herself from the table. Later that night as I was walking past Gorgeous' room, I heard crying. I knocked then walked in.
"What's wrong?" Gorgeous extended her arms, looked up with her tear stained face and said, "Hold me." She sounded like a helpless child. I got undressed, climbed in bed with her and she put her head on my chest and began to talk.

"When I was nine my step-father started touching me, performing oral sex on me and demanding it in return. One night he was drunk and he had his two guys with him. I was 13. They came into my room and ran a train on me all night. The next morning I was so sore I couldn't go to school. My mother took me to the hospital and the doctor kept me overnight. She told the doctor that I had been raped by two masked men. He explained to my mother how I could never have children because of the damage. My mother ignored it and said to me, "That's just how men are. Get use to it". My step-father continued fucking me on a regular basis until I was 15. I crept into his room one night with a knife and stabbed him in his dick. My mother had me sent to a mental institution. When I was released 10 months later, my mother and step-father had moved out of state. I had no where to go. I've been on my own ever since.

I haven't seen or heard from my mother since. Mickey, I've been selling pussy since I was 15. I lived on the streets until I was 18 then I joined the military. Where's my husband? Where are my kids? Don't you think I'd make a good wife, a good mother?"

"Sure you would."

She cried all night in my arms until she cried herself to sleep. Gorgeous was my best friend and I cared for her deeply. I had never heard of such tales of physical and sexual abuse until I started actually listening to these women. These knights of the night as I called them had dealt with rape and assault daily as an occupational hazard.

I recall a story Candy told me of when she was hooking in Oakland. She was robbed and sodomized at knife point. She viewed it as an occupational hazard, just part of the job. Afterwards she adjusted her clothes and make up and went back to work on the corner. Gorgeous wasn't damaged, she was destroyed. When something is destroyed, it's damaged beyond repair. Their abuse goes ignored because the scars are invisible to the naked eye.

We were awakened by the sound of Agent Murphy standing over me going through Gorgeous' drawers asking me questions.

"I helped you and you give me dick", said Murphy.

"You haven't helped me with shit. What do you want from me?"

"Sasquatch Ali! When he surfaces to get you, we'll nab him for the murder of Muhammad Salaam."

.

In my heart I knew Ali didn't do it. Besides I was piecing together this mystery myself. I had my own theories.

"Let me talk to you in private." said Murphy.

"You can speak in front of Gorgeous."

"Get out Honey" demanded Murphy. Gorgeous looked at me and I nodded, then she left the room.

Murphy handed me his card again and continued to talk over the sounds of sinful screams coming from two other rooms. "Call me when you see Ali. You owe me," said Murphy as he left out unconcerned with my new chosen profession.

Gorgeous walked back in as he left and crawled back in bed with me. "I remember when Momo died the whole city kinda mourned." Gorgeous said. Apparently, she'd been eavesdropping. I quickly changed the subject and then left the room.

Mickey Royal

Chapter Seven

Royal Flush

The money was pouring in. Purrfect was now my biggest asset. She took the initiative to install a 1-900 phone line in her home for phone-sex, using her own money, but still paying me my 40%. Purrfect leased a candy apple red Lincoln Town Car limousine with Royalty on the license plate. Baby Girl bought a green Lexus coupe with her own money but Purrfect made her exchange it for a candy apple red one.

Purrfect gave me the limo. "You're our King. You should ride like one" said Purrfect. Cliff became my full-time chauffeur. Now I only traveled by limo with Cliff at the wheel. I hired two more retired L.A.P.D. officers and placed one at each house.

I moved out and bought a condo in Fox Hills. By now all of the women had their own apartments. Of course, Purrfect owned her own house in Windsor Hills.

Purrfect was a dancer at night and a business major by day when I met her. She was a genius and a great asset to the family. The Royal Family was Mickey Royal, Purrfect, Baby Girl, Fantasy, Gorgeous, Candy and Cleopatra. The girls were only allowed to work in the house five days out of the seven. They could choose which five. I was running a marathon, not sprinting.

Purrfect spent more time advertising at clubs, bars, casinos, and on the computer than turning tricks. She printed a card with a group photo of the girl's pictures on it. The card read, "Royal Family Entertainment Professional Escorts, Extremely Discreet," with the phone number on the bottom. She even had the cards in travel agency catalogs.

I went by to see Aminah and Hussain. "Damn, you just the new king or something.

You pull up in a limousine and I'm working at Ralphs?"

"Look, that's why I'm here, I want to take care of you both" as I pointed to Hussain.

"I have a very nice two-bedroom condo in Fox Hills."

"Give me 30 minutes to pack," Aminah said as she took off her cashier's uniform, packed one suitcase and picked up Hussain. We left. She wrote Chris a thank you note and I left him $500.

Aminah, my four-year-old son and I decided to try again. We got to my place.

"You no longer have to work just raise Hussain and be my wife."

"What about your whores?"

"Those are my co-workers, and you'll have to respect them. Those whores, as you call them, take care of us. We work together and we are family, especially Gorgeous. So watch your mouth."

Aminah smiled and said, "Excuse me."

Aminah was happy to be back with me and happy to no longer be working. I had given Momo my word to protect his daughters. Fatimah was happily married and doing well. Even though I was pimping, I was still a gangster at heart. A true gangster, especially a Muslim, always keeps his word. I no longer loved Aminah but I loved Hussain and I felt an obligation to Momo, like a field sergeant to a general.

Aminah got in her place. She became the perfect little housewife. We started going out as a family to places. We were even making love again with the intensity of a teenage newlywed couple. Business was good and home was great. One morning I woke up to breakfast in bed with Hussain on my left, Aminah on my right and the remote control in my hand. That's when she just came out and said it.

"I'm pregnant."

"Are you sure?"

"Positive, Chris knows already, so does Fatimah."

I was happy. My first thought was that this would help solidify our relationship. I felt with Aminah and me back together Momo would have been proud. He had been like a father to me. I admired and respected him.

"Aminah?"

"Yes Mikail"

"How long have you known Ali?" I asked.

"All of my life. He was like the nanny. My father was always busy, but Ali was never too busy to spend time with us. He would be the one taking us to the movies, to school and tucking us in at night. My father was always meeting with someone somewhere. After my mom died, Ali moved in and did the cooking and cleaning. He loved my father like a son."

"Why?"

"Oh, just curious."

Two nights later I called Gorgeous and told her to organize a family picnic. Everyone showed up. Everyone brought something. Tony and Gorgeous bar-b-qued. We had the ghetto blaster blasting and we bumped everything from Tupac to Isaac Hayes.

I was happy to see Gorgeous and Aminah

some what getting along. Hussain had a connection with Baby Girl. She pushed him on the swings. We even had plenty of foil for leftovers. It was a real domestic scene. We drew lots of attention to ourselves; the pretty girls, the cars, the music, all of it.

Chris and Cleopatra were playing basketball. John Dough was there. He came with Tony Pleasure. John Dough was a bookie who headquartered himself in Tony's Beauty/Barber shop. I sat at the head of the cleanest picnic table, like Don Corleone and awaited John's proposal.

As John and Tony approached, instead of a cat on my lap, I had Baby Girl. Her legs didn't even touch the ground. Tony introduced us even though I knew who John was and Tony knew that. I had to have heard of him.

"Mickey this is John Dough. He's cool and he wanted to talk to you," said Tony. Gorgeous called for Baby Girl to come help her, but actually Gorgeous knew John and I were about to discuss something Baby Girl had no need to be hearing.

"Mickey Royal… It's an honor."

"Likewise"

"I have an idea for a quick flip. An after hours joint." I listened as he went on about it, but game recognizes game. I was the hottest thing on the streets and he needed a flag to work under. "Give me your number" I said. He gave me his card. John Dough Inc. his card read. He had kept it short and simple, then he left. John Dough was in his mid-thirties and he wasn't connected to any gang or clique. He was a hell of a bookie and would be a great asset to me.

We left the park late. Everyone left separately, but Baby Girl and Aminah rode with me in the limo. I was so sexually attracted to Baby Girl I could barely function in her presence, but I was strong enough to not let her know. We were in the limo with Aminah on my left, Hussain on my right and Baby Girl sitting directly across from me.

My name was Mickey Royal and I was the king. I was feeling as powerful as people were saying I was. Royal Family Entertainment was netting me 5 grand a day easy. With two houses and a "1-900" line my cut was now 40% across the board.

Purrfect had the girls doing bachelor parties, but with two conditions. The conditions were that they had to order two or more girls and that the cash had to be up front. Not including tips. Purrfect organized a car wash in a shopping center parking lot. All of the girls wore swimsuits and flirted with the customers. Purrfect didn't wash cars. She set up a hot dog stand and worked it. Gorgeous didn't wash cars either. She walked back and forth up and down the sidewalk holding the car wash sign. All the money made was donated to the U.N.C.F. That also was Purrfect's idea. I drove by the car wash and the girls playfully bowed. Cliff honked the horn and I rolled down the window and gave them the thumbs up.

The U.N.C.F. received a check from Royal Family Entertainment for $5,000. Of course, we didn't make 5,000 that day. I added most of it from my own pocket to make the check worth receiving.

A week later I called a meeting, a private meeting at Chris's place.

In Chris's living room sat the key players; Chris, John Dough, Gorgeous and myself. I went around the room and introduced everyone.

"Here's the deal John. I want you to set up all forms of gambling upstairs. I mean craps, cards, sports you name it. Chris, you can run loan sharking and narcotics weed only, and Gorgeous, you'll work primarily downstairs with the girls and drinks."

"Mickey, what are you talking about?" asked John.

"An after-hours club," said Gorgeous, answering for me. That was that. We shook hands in agreement and then we all left.

We drove to the storefront I had rented and looked things over. The outside was white with a black iron screen door. Gorgeous put the word out that we would open in five days and all of the girls had to come every night. John and I talked about the set-up.

John, Chris and I spent the next few days setting up the after hours. We put a sign outside the club that read: Royal Flush Social Club. The social club part was for the cops, to have a 'legitimate' use for the storefront.

Opening night came and it was packed. Our hours were from 1:00am to 6:00am. Just 5 hours a day. Gorgeous and Purrfect still had influence with the dancers at Monte Carlo as well as other clubs and were able to pull them. Because Monte's closed at 2:00am and the girls who danced at Monte Carlo, Mae Westside, and those that wanted extra money came to Royal Flush.

Gorgeous was opening night's door greeter wearing her trademark black and gold silk lingerie set with matching garter belt and a loosely tied trench coat. After you made it past Gorgeous you entered the lounge area outfitted with vending machines, pool tables and couches. Behind the lounge area was a stage for totally nude dancing and areas for lap dancing.

Royal Flush Social Club only cost ten bucks to get in and drinks were regular priced. Separating the lounge from the dancing area were curtains.

You walk through the curtains and enter the main room where the stage is. In addition to the stage is a bar. At the back of the room, by the restroom is a staircase.

Upstairs were craps, no-limit hold-em poker, sports books and blackjack tables. John Dough ran the upstairs. In the far corner he sat at his desk where he took bets on sports. He had the spread sheet on a chalkboard behind him. He paid me 5,000 up front and 40% of the take. Craps was the big money maker. Royal Flush netted 17,000 the first night and held steady at 15 grand a day net. Chris sold marijuana and cigarettes up and downstairs. I also got 40% of that take. Chris didn't have to buy in though. Since we went way back together I waved that fee.

The girls, non-Royal Family hookers, would sit in the lobby and wait to be picked. The ladies would pay $35 to get in and work the lobby. There were always at least 20 girls working. The Royal Family, my girls, would alternate the nights they worked. Gorgeous worked every night.

I would take the cash at the end of the night, which would be about 7am. We would count and divide the cash according to the appropriate percentages. Then I would take the cash to a safe deposit box at the bank.

Gorgeous would bring in high rollers. Gorgeous was great at it. With her 6-foot stature, she attracted men, women and couples. I would have thought Gorgeous would have been jealous of all of the authority I gave to Purrfect, but she wasn't. Instead, her jealousy was directed at Baby Girl. One morning as I was sleeping in my wife's arms, Purrfect called me at home no less.

"Come get yo bitch, Mickey. She's tripping and she's fucking up today's business."

"What's she doing?"

"Right now, she's choking Baby Girl!"

"Where's security?" I asked.

"They're scared to touch her. She says she'll have them fired", said Purrfect.

When I got there Gorgeous, who was drunk, was cursing. Baby Girl was scared and packing.

"I quit.... I don't need this shit!" Baby Girl screamed in my face. I told Purrfect to calm Baby Girl down and had security physically put Gorgeous out. "What's the matter with you?" I asked. Gorgeous just drove away without answering.

Purrfect said the right things to Baby Girl to keep her, thank god. Aminah started paging me so I went right back home to find Agent Murphy in my refrigerator and Aminah sitting on the couch. Hussain was still asleep.

"Why are you here?" I asked Agent Murphy. "I told you...I'm on the Salaam case. You've given me nothing to go on. My sources say Ali is alive. Since you won't help me, I will no longer help you" said Murphy.

"What's that supposed to mean. What help?" I asked in an argumentative aggressive tone. Murphy simply stormed out.

The next day it was business as usual at Palace 1 and 2. The money was still pouring in and everybody was happy. That night I was at the Royal Flush checking on my game, being the perfect host, occasionally gambling. I even won 60 bucks on the crap table. That was when I heard a loud crashing sound.

I reached for my .357 Magnum then dropped it when I saw cops. Why? Because that's how so-called accidents happen with the L.A.P.D.

It was a raid. The cops totally wrecked the place. I mean with malicious intent. They did unnecessary shit like smashed up the vending machines that I was renting no doubt. They even knew just who to arrest. They seized tonight's take and took me, John, Chris, and Gorgeous. Everyone else was just told to leave immediately.

I was handcuffed and put in the back of a squad car. While down at the police station I worried for Gorgeous. Because she was female she was separated from the rest of us. In the holding tank the common criminal couldn't believe that he had the honor of being locked up with Mickey Royal and John Dough.

"A cuz", one of them said. I turned to him and said, "You talking to me?" Then he asked,

"You Mickey Royal?"

"Yep."

Then as I walked over to sit down, the group of accused gentlemen on the bench parted like the Red Sea. I sat down but John continued to pace. After eight hours, with no food or phone call, in came a guard.

"Sharif, Davis (John Dough's real last name), Goodwin (Chris Good's last name), let's go!"

John, Chris and I were released. Gorgeous was given a phone call and used it to call the Palace. Purrfect and Cliff came to pick us up in the limo. Ironically, Gorgeous wasn't released until two hours later. I was there by myself to get her in a cab.

"We weren't even charged" Gorgeous said. I didn't answer. Right now I had no idea who I could really trust. We took a cab to Norma's restaurant. Gorgeous gave the waitress a five-dollar tip. She always tipped before her meal came. I felt Gorgeous was the only one I could possibly trust.

"I talked to Candy and she said the girls are nervous. They smell defeat Mickey," Gorgeous said. .“And you…what do you smell?” I replied. Gorgeous stared into my empty, completely confident eyes and slowly smiled.

“Pancakes, I smell delicious blueberry pancakes!”

I smiled back and we began to eat. I was starving. However, I didn’t want to ignore her fear of the Royal Family’s destruction. I had to address it. “Gorgeous, gather all the girls tonight. We’re gonna have a little meeting.” I then temporarily excused myself and went to the phone.

I knew Agent Murphy was behind that raid, but I wanted to know why I we weren’t charged. I couldn’t find his card so I called the police station directly. “Yea, let me speak to Agent Murphy, it’s urgent!” The cop paused and replied,

“There is no Agent Murphy that works here.” I hung up quickly.

I went back to the table and kept my new found info to myself. Murphy was obviously apart of a different government agency, but who? We finished eating and left. That night I organized a kind of farewell to the Royal Flush. “We’re gonna roll down Crenshaw in parade fashion.

We'll roll from Crenshaw and King Blvd, starting behind Magic's Theater to Crenshaw and Rosecrans. Then a left up Rosecrans to Monte Carlo's in Gardena"

"Monte told me not ever show my face there again", said Gorgeous trembling in fear.

"I'll handle Monte and you're with me." I said to Gorgeous as I watched the look on her face go from worried to calm. I left with Cliff in my limo and the girls left one at a time after me.

When I got home Aminah was sleep but Hussain was up watching Cartoon Network, so I made him a snack and joined him. We both fell asleep on the couch. When I woke up Aminah had covered us up with a blanket. Aminah and I were getting along fine. Fremont had humbled her.

"Aminah, start looking for a house" I said to her as I woke up on the couch. Her face lit up, "Okay, when are we moving?"

"Sometime this month" I replied. She became very happy with this announcement.

Over the next few days we went house shopping. I was leaning toward a three-bedroom, two bath house in Inglewood where I grew up. Aminah was looking in the View Park and Ladera Heights area. The house I chose went for $375,000. The house she picked cost $625,000. I wanted to please her but I couldn't fill her father's shoes, not yet. I had close to $650,000 in cash in a safe deposit box. I had about $50,000 in the bank 'legitimately' earned by Royal Family Entertainment that was in my personal account. I had about $225,000 in the Royal Family Inc account.

Aminah was always comparing me to her father but I wasn't Momo. She wasn't trying to break me, she was just trying to get her life back, the one she had before I entered it. I had to get that house. That house represented more than just a house to her.

So I took $200,000 out of the Royal Family account and put it down on the house. I knew I couldn't really afford it but I couldn't afford not to buy it. It made her so happy. I gave her $30,000 out of the safe deposit and let her fill the new place with furniture. She picked out things and decorated the house as close to her home growing up as possible, right down to the exercise equipment in the garage. So we started to pack.

Agent Murphy came by the town house during one of our family bonding moments. The doorbell rang. I answered the door. It was Murphy. "You and I need to talk" I said as I walked out of the door and closed it behind me. We walked to the street and I laid into him.

"Who are you?" I asked. He turned, looked at me and said,

"What do you mean?"

"I couldn't find your number, so I called the police station looking for you. They said that they had never heard of you. But yet, when the L.A.P.D. arrested me for assault, it was you who interviewed me about Momo and Ali and you had your own office at the station. Now again who are you?"

"I'm with the FBI. Salaam was one of ours" said Murphy with the tone of defeat.

"Bullshit!" I replied as I turned to go inside.

He grabbed me and said, "Listen! Don't you find it odd that Jamal is doing life without parole and Salaam wasn't and yet they were charged with the same crime?

How do you think that Salaam got out early? Now look. Ali killed Salaam and we're looking for him. We need to know what Salaam told him. Ali needs to be detained, debriefed and interrogated. We've watched every move you've made since you first hit that jeweler's house. We've been protecting you since you got back to the city. We've helped you along in your criminal career without you knowing, hoping that you got infamous enough to draw Ali out of hiding" said Murphy.

"So all I was all along was bait?" I asked.

"Yes Mikail, for a really big fish. Now, here's my card, again! Please call me if he shows up" said Murphy. Then he left. I walked back in stunned by what I had just heard. "Baby, you okay? You look like somebody died" said Aminah. Somebody had died…a part of me. I didn't want to believe it but I knew it could be true. But there are two sides to every coin. I held back my emotions and continued to pack.

Tonight was the night. We all loaded up in our candy apple red cars and began the Royal parade, with the limo in the rear. Gorgeous' Navigator was first. We drove in a straight line down Crenshaw to the sound of people cheering and horns honking. As we drove past Leimert Park I knew I was saying goodbye, at least for the moment.

I didn't mind saying goodbye. I had come back to the city dirt poor and had risen to power in just under two years. So even though the Royal Empire was hitting a few bumps at the time as we rode, I still felt I had won. I finally felt I had closure on a criminal career that I had started in the summer of 1986 at the tender age of 13. I first made my 'bones' that summer.

I felt as though I finally had something to show for two stab wounds, a bullet hole, all of the jail time, the work I put in, Fremont, the humiliation, everything. It all felt worth it as Gorgeous led the way with a left turn on Rosecrans, headed toward Monte Carlo's in Gardena. We all walked in together, without paying.

Gorgeous had on a full-length mink coat with a tiara like a beauty queen. She walked in with me arm and arm as my queen. The dancers were happy to see Gorgeous and Purrfect again.

Lamont came out of the back to congratulate me on the success of the Royal Family. I hadn't seen him in months. He shook my hand and said, "The King" in a sarcastic manner. Then he asked "Who's that short red bone?"

"Baby Girl" I replied.

"Hook me up nigga."

"No problem"

This was our little way of making up. We've known each other our entire lives and we go back too far to hold any long, serious grudges.

But it was blatantly Gorgeous' night. She was the queen of the scene. The DJ pointed to her and put her song on which was Funky Lady (Foxy

Lady) by Slave. As she made her way to the stage one of the younger dancers at Monte Carlo's named Passion (who was 19 but 21 on her fake I.D) yelled out "Don't hurt yourself!" Gorgeous smiled and answered, "Watch and learn child, class is in session."

Gorgeous was 20 to 25 years older than the average dancer in the club. Dancers dance to a beat but Gorgeous was so much of a pro, it looked as if the beat was designed to her movements. Watching her dance was time stopping pleasure. As I watched her take Passion's little young ass to school on that stage I was overwhelmingly proud. In that moment Gorgeous taught me the difference between a stripper and an Exotic Dancer.

Gorgeous was in the zone. The zone where instinct takes over and the soul flies. If you've ever seen Muhammad Ali box, Florence Griffith-Joyner run, or Michael Jackson on stage then you know the zone I speak of. The zone when you're at the right place and time doing what you were born to do.

Lamont walked up to the front of the stage

while Gorgeous was 'zoned out' and put a C-note in her garter, then went back to his office. I was so afraid he was going to wreck her zone to the point where I had my hand on my gun. I was prepared to shoot him here and now if he had ruined her mood. That's when I realized the obvious.

I was in love with Gorgeous. She was my best-friend and the only one I completely trusted. Well, her and Tony. I was totally in love with her six-foot Amazonian frame, her charm and magnetic personally. I wanted her in my life for the rest of it. I felt like Judas the Betrayer. Gorgeous has had my back from day one, but it's the adulterous Aminah who got the house. Something about that didn't seem right.

Just then Gorgeous came off the stage to stand close to me, by my side. The crowd was still cheering and Passion was in awe of my Gorgeous. "Mustafa's outside in a limo. He wants to see you" a bouncer said to me. A sudden coldness came over my soul. I didn't know what to expect. It's been over six years.

Gorgeous could sense trouble in the air. She could also see the look of fear on my face. I looked at Gorgeous and said, "Wait here. I'll be back."

To my surprise, Gorgeous followed me outside right up to the limousine door. "Gorgeous, go back inside" I said. But she wouldn't budge. One of Mustafa's bodyguards got out of the back of the limo and frisked me, removing my gun. I was scared, but being from the street and choosing the life I had chosen, I understood how the game was played. Win, lose or draw, you take your medicine.

"Let's go for a ride" said the bodyguard directly to me. Gorgeous but in and said, "Oh goodie I like rides." Gorgeous then tried to enter the limo ahead of me but Mustafa's bodyguard grabbed her by the elbow, pulling her back. She snatched away from him and screamed "Get yo fuckin hands off me nigga! Wherever Mickey goes I go. What happens to him happens to me" she said with fearless authority. Gorgeous saw that they wanted me to ride alone and weren't going to let her in the car. "I'll be okay" I said to her with a nod of confidence. “Look…uhm.. ah I’m going back inside. Call me if you need me. Come here, gimmie a hug!” said Gorgeous. Gorgeous, knowing I was unarmed and unprotected hugged me around my waist on the inside of my trench coat.

She slipped her trademark .22 caliber two shot Derringer in my back right pocket, kissed me on the top of my head and whispered, “Be careful” as I whispered back, “Always.” Gorgeous turned around and strutted back into the club and I got into Mustafa’s limo.

“Long time no see” I said to Mustafa as the limo pulled off. “Can you imagine what it’s like not to be able to walk?” said Mustafa referring to his paralysis. “I heard about your misfortune. What happened?”

“Momo and I were about to go to war, dig? But I didn’t feel as though it was all that serious so me and one of my boys went to his pad. I was gonna to talk to him man-to-man and come to some sort of truce. I was gonna even cut him in 15% of my end of the deal. His garage door was up and no one was in there. When I walked in his garage where the weights were I heard a shot. I pulled my pistol and a dude came running out the door that connects the garage and the house with a gun in his hand, running straight at me.

So I shot him. As I turned to run back to my car, I heard another shot and fell on my stomach. I felt a warm, numbing sensation in my back. My boy hopped out of the car and dragged me into the car. But whoever shot me came out of the house afterwards because the nigga I shot was D.O.A."

"How do you know he was D.O.A?" I asked.

"Because I saw his brains hit the floor" he answered. Mustafa leaned over, rubbed his toothpick like legs and continued. "Let's get to the point of my visit.

The only reason you're not dead is because I've learned you can't collect money from dead people. You owe me $20,000 from the Mississippi Slick pick up and another $100,000 or so in interest."

"That was six years ago. I don't even remember all

that." Right then the window separating us and the driver rolled down and the bodyguard in the front passenger seat put a gun to my head.

Mustafa touched my knee and said "You have 24 hours." The bodyguard with the gun put it back in his suit and rolled up the dividing window.

"What if I found out who shot you?"

"Was it you?" asked Mustafa with a raised eyebrow.

"No, it wasn't."

"Well I'd kill him immediately!" said Mustafa.

Mustafa then gave me his phone number and told me to call him if I ever found out. Mustafa and I talked for another ten minutes about the music business. Mustafa owns a very successful record company.

He no longer deals directly with anything illegal of any kind. Apparently being shot made him re-direct his life. The Mustafa I had known six years ago was a fearless hot head. This man, this Mustafa was quiet, patient and soft-spoken.

This new Mustafa, in my opinion was far more

dangerous. Mustafa's record label is growing and I had to say I was impressed. He had signed some big named acts.

He told me that Lamont, my childhood chum, was a major manufacturer of marijuana. He stated that Lamont has garages and empty houses all along Highway I-5, from L.A. to Seattle filled with marijuana plants. This is the same Lamont that I've been disrespecting and testing.

Mustafa told me Lamont is one of the biggest marijuana suppliers in Los Angeles. He only does deals in the six- figure range. After our conversation I still had little to no respect for Lamont. Mustafa acts as sort of a mentor to Lamont. He's taught Lamont to keep a low profile. I knew then that Lamont was Mustafa's biggest earner and that's why he wears that ring all of the time.

Mustafa's limo dropped me back off at the club, but the club was now closed. The parking lot was empty. I called Cliff to come pick me up and I went home. When I woke up I called Mustafa to come and pick up his 120 grand. Only 10 hours had passed from the time he dropped me off at Monte Carlo's.

Chapter Eight

The Clock Strikes Twelve

Lying in the bed, looking up at the ceiling at home, I finally started putting it together. I got up and got dressed, called Cliff to pick me up and left out the house in search of truth and closure. It was starting to clear up.

I was remembering what Murphy said how you think Momo got out so early. In a flash, I ordered Cliff to make a U-turn. I had him drop me off in Watts in front of the Diamond Pawn Shop. As soon as Cliff was out of sight, I called Gorgeous on her cell phone.

"Gorgeous, do me a big favor. I'm at Diamond's Pawn Shop in Watts. Pull in front and wait for me."

"I'm on my way."

I walked in, browsed around until the last customer left.

"Benjamin, talk to me."

"What's on your mind kid?"

"How did Momo get out of jail?"

"I told you. My family got him out. My uncle was his lawyer."

"Was Momo an agent?" Ben looked at me with shock and said "Absolutely not!" I punched him in the stomach and he answered with a pretty good right cross of his own. Before I knew it we had grabbed on to each other, both of us hitting the floor punching on the way down.

"Don't fuck with me. I need the truth!" I screamed. Ben started gasping for air and he was trying to tell me something. "Medicine" he whispered, and then he pointed to the counter. Behind the counter I found his asthma inhaler. I gave it to him. I locked the door and flipped the Open sign on the door to Closed. I put my pistol to his chest. Ben was still on the floor at the time, trying to catch this breath.

Even with a gun to his chest he refused to talk.

Ben was old school blood and guts and didn't scare easily. I saw he had no fear of me so I appealed to his humanity. "Mr. Diamond, the F.B.I. comes around everyday and harasses Aminah and me. Help me. Please!" I pleaded to him.

"Those pricks harass little Aminah, for what?"

"They think that I'm holding out on the Momo murder and Ali's whereabouts." Ben began getting up off of the floor slowly and I reached down to help him up. I put the gun on his counter close to him to show trust. That now he held the power and I was totally at his mercy.

Mr. Diamond poured a cup of espresso from his machine and began to pace and talk. He was nervous, his hands were trembling and he was looking around.

"They harass Aminah?"

"Daily when I'm not home."

If Murphy was right, then I knew that Ben would know. A deal of such magnitude would have to be approved by a lawyer. If Murphy was right, then I knew that the deal was negotiated by Momo's lawyer...Ben's uncle. Mr. Diamond paced a little more and began to speak.

"We were kids, two Negroes and a Jew. We stuck out like a sore thumb. We were a crew, right out here on these streets in Watts after the riots and after we left the war. Times were different then.

We met in Vietnam. We were in the same unit. It was in the jungles of Vietnam when the three of us decided to form a pact. When we got out of the marines we dove right into it. We were involved in a little of everything but mostly little heists. When we were in our twenties we pulled a bank job. It was a major score, but something went wrong, and shooting started.

Jamal had killed a cop and before we knew it we were all caught. There was no death penalty in California at the time so we received the max. Jamal received a 100 year sentence. Muhammad got a 50-year sentence and I received a lighter 15 years for two reasons. Number one, because I was white and with no prior convictions, unlike Muhammad and

Jamal and two, I never got out of the car.

It just so happened on this run I was the wheel man." He took another sip of espresso and continued. "I served my time, 9 ½ in the joint. Momo was pressuring my family and me to get him out. He couldn't do the time. He knew he would die in prison. He'd begun going stir crazy and even started hallucinating. My entire family stuck by his side. Appeals, parole hearings you name it, we were there. Then three and a half years after my release the FBI approached my uncle with a deal. It was a secret deal that would guarantee Salaam's release immediately. It would also guarantee that Muhammad Salaam would never do another day in prison no matter what the charge. He would be given total immunity for the rest of his life. My uncle and Salaam discussed it and Salaam agreed. They bought his soul."

"What are you talking about…I don't understand. What? You mean voodoo shit?" I responded sarcastically. "No nothing like that. Salaam and Jamal had formed Al-Ossrah while in prison and it grew in those ten years. As it grew and attracted the attention of Washington D.C. Salaam was released and the deal was his tombstone.

The FBI offered him a second chance. A second chance is priceless Sharif. Salaam was back on the streets with a huge reputation and an assignment for his second chance.

His assignment was to infiltrate what was left of the Black Panther Party. Because of his rep and community stature, he was trusted by the Panther Party and elevated to a high position. But it was his secretly taped conversations and information that lead to hundreds of arrests and political assassinations." "No" I said in a soft voice with tears in my eyes. I had no foundation strong enough to support what I was hearing. Ben continued.

"Momo then started recruiting immediately. Since he knew he had the immunity status of a diplomat. The feds had Momo dealing drugs in the community and they would bust the other dealers who dealt with him." I kept shaking my head in denial "Bullshit!" I screamed. "He was what is known as a 'plant.' When his conscience started getting the best of him he threatened to quit.

The Feds said that they would make it public knowledge that Momo was a snitch and let the folks in the community deal with him. So he had no choice but to continue. By now Momo was in so deep he couldn't turn around. Then he met a woman, Bernadette. They wed and had the twins, Aminah and Fatimah." I was listening with absolute undivided attention. I just sat there listening forgetting all about Gorgeous sitting outside waiting on me.

Benjamin looked at me with eyes of sorrow and said, "He loved her, and because he wanted her to be able to respect him, he quit dealing dope and working for the F.B.I. He had walked away. He stopped checking in and tried to move his family elsewhere.

A week later Bernadette was found hanging in the bathroom of their home. The police ruled it a suicide, but I for one never believed it.

That was around the time when he hired that Ali character and they hit it off. Remember when I told you the story almost a year ago about Ali?"

"Yea. I remember," I replied.

"Those cops weren't cops, they were Feds dressed as cops. They and Momo were working together. That beating was staged. Whenever rumors circulated of Momo's co-operation something like that had to be done. That beating was masterful PR.

When Momo gave information it would have been too risky for him to just walk into headquarters with a file in his hand. What if someone saw him? So to avoid that, the cops would arrest him in front of his crew and they could then get the information in private. Ali had no idea of any of this. When he killed the two Feds he was just trying to protect his boss.

When he did that the Feds had to let it go. They couldn't charge him. They figured the operation was more important that just two Feds. That was just more to hang on Momo if he ever wanted to quit again. Sharif, the reason Crips and

Bloods stayed away from Momo's action was because people who dealt with Momo somehow ended up dead or in jail."

By now, Gorgeous gotten impatient and my pager was going off. Aminah was paging me. I left the pawn shop without saying a word and got in the Navigator with Gorgeous.

"What's going on, Mickey?" asked Gorgeous. Before I could answer, the cops pulled us over and I was arrested. I told Gorgeous to go and see about Aminah. I knew what they wanted. Agent Murphy was in the car.

"Look Sharif. How does this sound to you?" asked Murphy with a smile on his face.

"1992 breaking and entering, robbery and assault. You remember that jewelry job. Accomplice to the murder of Mississippi Slick, assault on a man with a crowbar, two counts of murder on Imperial Highway in 92, not to mention Royal Flush, money laundering, racketeering. Good God boy, you're looking at life, unless you play ball."

Then Murphy continued to explain how that

evidence could all get lost if I was willing to replace it with anything I knew about Mustafa, Lamont or Ali. To buy time, I told him that I would see what I could do. Murphy smiled at me and stated, "We look forward to working with you." Then the car stopped and they let me out at home. I called up Mustafa from my house.

"Mustafa I know who killed Momo."

"So what, who gives a fuck?"

"And I also know who shot you."

"What's your address? I'm on my way."

Gorgeous was still at the house with Aminah and Hussain. "Gorgeous, when Mustafa gets here, they're going to follow us."

"Follow us where?"

"To the beginning of the end."

I didn't tell her specifically because Aminah was standing right beside her. I had no secrets from Gorgeous.

Mustafa and his people pulled up in two black 600 V12 Mercedes Benz, armed to the teeth. Gorgeous and I were downstairs waiting to meet them. They arrived. I walked up to the window, leaned in, made eye contact with Mustafa and said; "Look Mustafa, follow us over there. Wait until Gorgeous and I come out and drive off before y'all go in." When we pulled up, Mustafa and his people waited outside just like I asked. "I'll owe you one" said Mustafa as he shook my hand.

We pulled up then I went in and confronted him. "How y'all doing?" asked Chris as Gorgeous and I entered his apartment. Chris sat on his couch and I started in on him. "Why? Why did you kill your uncle?" Chris laughed and said, "What? Are you high?"

"No, but try this on for size. I've been talking to Ben Diamond and I know about the deal."

"I don't know about any deal."

"Aminah told you everything that went on in that house and you used that information. Two different guns were used, one on the guy in the garage and one on Momo and the guard in the house. After Momo's wife was killed, he went back to work for the Feds.

Ali used to watch the girls for ten days a month while Momo was out of the country setting up offshore accounts. He was planning to take his girls and run. He wasn't preparing for war with Mustafa or Jamal. He was trying to take his family and disappear. The Feds found out he was planning to quit again and Momo remembered what happened to his wife, so he asked if you knew anybody who could protect his girls and you brought me in.

You knew I would have said no so you set up that jewelry thing. That's why Momo knew nothing of the jewels when he and I met. You just used that to suck me in. Momo wanted me to watch his girls in case of an attack.

He knew he couldn't trust anyone in Al-Ossrah to watch his girls. He knew there was a spy or leak somewhere and he didn't know who to trust. There's only one way to be sure not to pick a bad apple out of the barrel, and that was by picking it off of the tree."

"I don't know shit about no Feds or any bullshit like

that. But what makes you think I did it?" I went on to say, "Momo wasn't trying to protect his daughters from Mustafa. Al-Ossrah doesn't hit women or children and I was guarding the twins before the Mustafa drama started.

When that carload of guys pulled up to kill me on Imperial, I noticed they pointed their guns at the back seat. The twins were the target, not me. No one but Momo, Ali, you and I knew where the twins were going."

"Ali could have tipped them off."

"No, because only you knew exactly where Tony lived. That car was waiting for us. They knew we'd be coming sooner or later. It was an ambush. Momo was killed in his sleep.

He had to have known and trusted his assassin. You waited until Momo went to sleep, then you shot him. Next you shot the inside guard. The outside guard ran in and must have seen you, then ran back out of the house.

That man met the bitter end at the surprise of Mustafa's gun. Mustafa turned to run and you, who were chasing the guy out of the house, saw Mustafa and shot him in the back. Then you went out the back way."

"Why?"

"He never gave me nothing. He always treated me like some outside flunky. He treated you like the son he never had after just a few months of knowing you. I saw him give a suitcase full of money to Ali and he wished him well. We got into it that night. He and I almost came to blows. We argued all night about my mother and he referred to me as an unimportant mistake. I pulled out a gun and he laughed. He just laughed at me, turned his back and went to sleep."

"Did Mustafa know? Was he in on it?"

"No. I never even met Mustafa."

"So that made you kill your own uncle?"

"He wasn't my uncle Mr. know-it-all. He was my father!" My mouth just dropped. It turned 'Aunt Sylvia wasn't Momo's sister as he had told his daughters and wife Bernadette , she was his mistress and Chris' mom. The hate made more sense now. "The twins don't even know. No one knew but me, my mom and Momo. I was supposed to be a secret. But one day my mom came over and got into it right at the door with Bernadette. My mother told Aunt Bernie everything. How he had two families. How Bernie was just a naive fool. The next thing I knew Momo and Aunt Bernie separated. When they got back together she kept throwing it up in his face. He had a ton of hookers on the side.

Bernadette already suffered from bi-polar disorder. She was already clinically depressed and couldn't take it anymore and one day just hung herself. She even left a suicide note. When I was a teenager Momo used to blame me for the death of his wife. He used to refer to her as his real wife, right to my face, like I asked to be born. Fuck Momo, I should have done it sooner."

"Why are you telling me all of this now?" I asked.

"Why not tell you? What difference will it make? Who you supposed to be nigga? You ain't nobody. How many days you think you'll have left?"

"I don't know"

I answered shrugging my shoulders being sarcastic and showing him I could honestly care less. "Where are you gonna go?" I asked Chris.

"Go? Nowhere,..It's my time now and I do what the green tells me."

"Money or envy" I angrily retorted. Chris gave me a stare I'll never forget. The look in his eyes at that moment told his entire story. I pitied Chris.

He had been so consumed with jealousy and envy for so long that it had festered into an intense bitter hatred for Salaam. A hatred so deeply rooted that the very subject of Momo angers Chris, even when discussing his demise.

"You coveted him so much you wanted to be him. You wanted his house, his cars, his F.B.I. protection his street clout, didn't you?" I said.

"What F.B.I. protection?"

That was when Gorgeous pulled me by the arm and we left. As we got into the Navigator and drove off, I could see in the rearview about four to five guys run up to Chris' front door and force their way inside which was followed by automatic gunfire. I knew at that point Chris was dead.

I actually felt sorry for Chris for a moment. I also felt guilty for setting him up. I had thought I was getting revenge for Momo and I felt strong about turning Chris over to Mustafa. But after these new revelations I realized that Chris was just another fatherless little boy in search of his lost manhood, like so many others.

On the way home I told Gorgeous the entire story. I wanted her to know this straight from my mouth to show my trust of her and just in case I got killed soon I wanted her to know this story and to take care of my wife and son. There was no one left. Gorgeous just drove in silence, listening as I talked to her.

"I told you this just in case something happens to me. Two days later I saw on CNN that 'Special Agent Allan Murphy was named assistant Director of the NSA.' I then knew strings were still being pulled because puppets were still dancing.

I went to visit Jamal in prison, alone.

They brought him in shackled, then un-cuffed him to let him talk on the phone. He sat down, smiled at me, picked up the phone and began to speak.

"Oh what a tangled web we weave when first we practice to deceive. All of those men fighting over something that belongs to me."

"What men?"

"Mustafa, Salaam, the government you name it. Everyone wants something from Al-Ossrah, but Al-Ossrah belongs to me. How can you control the tide when the ocean is mine? You can't! All you can do is ride the wave and pray it takes you where you wish to go. Once you hop on to that surfboard you are at the mercy of the ocean!"

"Where's Ali?"

"None of your business. He and Salaam's money are together living happily ever after. I always have my eyes and ears close to what I want to see and hear.

Don't look surprised young man. I can get close to anyone, anywhere right from in here. Even you" said Jamal as he gave me a look of the cat that had just swallowed the canary. "Don't worry, you'll be safe. Operation Salaam is closed. I will always be indebted to you for what you've done.

I want you to consider me your guardian angel."

"What about all that shit Murphy was saying to me about me being stuck and he having evidence on me?"

"Murphy was last of that old COINTELPRO crowd. J Edgar Hoover's COINTELPRO operation is pretty much closed now. If the government uses any evidence against you, then they would have to explain how they got it to the Grand Jury. And Operation Salaam was never approved. Plus, they would have to explain why they protected and supplied Salaam with drugs. The bottom line is narcotics earn an estimated 100 billion dollars a year in America. And Uncle Sam wants and will get his cut by any means necessary."

Visiting time was up and I had to go. "What have we learned today boys and girls?" asked Jamal. Then he smiled. "I learned that you're the puppet master." Jamal smiled again and said, "Am I?" He then hung up the phone and raised his arms to be re-shackled. On the way home I stopped off at my safe deposit box and got the rest of my money. I had about $480,000 in there. I also put another 70 grand in another safe in my closet just in case. When it comes to large illegal amounts of cash I kept it spread out just in case of a bust or raid, the cops won't have it all.

I walked in with $400,000 in a brown suitcase to find Gorgeous standing in the kitchen. She had gone through all of the drawers and cabinets looking for the stash.

"What are you looking for Gorgeous?"

"My cab is on its way. I want my cut. I need it. I gotta go! I kicked in 100%. I never kept a dime. I did my part and helped you build an empire. I need 50 grand. It's only fair."

"All this time I thought we were a team, you were working for yourself the whole time."

"We were, I mean are a team. I saw an opportunity and I took it."

"What?"

"Mickey, you're the sweetest, smartest, strongest man I've ever known. I've brought nothing but pain to the men I've known. Everyone I've ever loved I've lost. Everyone who's ever loved me I've destroyed. Would you leave Aminah for me?"

"Yes, I love you. I need you in my life." I replied and then I said, "And I know you love me."

She got angry and said, "Nigga, you don't even know me. You only know the bitch I introduced you to. Don't you think if I loved you, you would have at least known my real name? Mickey, it was all a game. That's what I do. I separate men from their money. I'm a pro." She looked me right in the face and saw the pain in my heart. "Don't do this Mickey." Her cab had pulled up. She ran outside and gave him a twenty and told him to wait. She then ran back into the house.

"We built something, The Royal Family is real. You and me, Mickey. We did this from the ground up. But you don't need me."

"I'll never forget you. I guess it was all a game.

That night you told me that bullshit story about your stepfather and your mother and then cried to sleep in my arms. You had me fooled, right down to the fake ass tears" I said.

I then opened my brown suitcase, counted out $200,000 in twenty stacks of ten grand, all C-notes and put them in the suitcase she was carrying. And she was only carrying one. She then gave me the Navigator keys. I turned around to walk in the kitchen. "Lock the door behind you" I said angrily. As I walked away, I heard her say, "My name is Tiffany Watkins. I was born November 10th, 1958 in Gary, Indiana. I was raised in Oakland California"

She walked up to me, kissed me, took my pinky ring from off my finger and placed on her gold chain around her neck.

"I'll never forget you either Mikail (finally she pronounced my name correctly)."

She picked up her suitcase. "Oh, and Mickey, about that night I cried myself to sleep in your arms, those tears were real." She let her head drop for a few seconds then she was out of the door and out of my life, just as mysteriously as she had entered it.

"Let's go suga," she said to the cab driver as she was getting into the cab. Just like that she was back in character. I watched her leave with an empty heart from the window. As the cab driver was putting her suitcase in the trunk I could see tears coming down her face. She looked back at me, kissed my ring, flipped her hair and got into her cab. Then she was gone. I found a note she left for me in her room.

It read:

Goodbye Mickey. Sorry to leave like this but I told you I never stay long enough anywhere to leave a footprint. Be good to Aminah, Hussain and the new baby to come. Aminah lost her father, cousin and her mother behind bullshit. She has no one but you. She needs you. I'll be okay. Don't try to find me because you won't be able to. You'll always be in what's left of my heart. I Love You.
Sincerely
Tiffany Watkins a.k.a. Gorgeous.

I never told Aminah the truth about Chris or Momo. I just couldn't. I figured what could be gained by exposure. As for me, I downsized first. I let the girls have their cars. I bought myself a Cadillac and Aminah a Lexus coupe. I put $100,000 in a safe deposit box just in case.

Mustafa said he owed me one, so I gave him $100,000 cash and he gave me back a check for $90,000, all clean. Lamont was buying Club Mae Westside, so I gave him that check to buy in for 35%. Tony and I are starting a management company. With his experience in music and my street connections, we'll do fine.

Aminah and I fought constantly in Fremont. Gorgeous electrified my soul and I'll always love her. But she was right; she was in too deep in the game. I know Tiffany Watkins a.k.a. Gorgeous loved me as much as she could have loved anyone. I could feel it. But in her world love is a liability, not an asset.

But that woman made me so happy. Her smile, her sense of humor and the intense times we spent together I will never forget. To this day I think about her every night.

Like tonight; as I look out over L.A. from my balcony I wonder where she is. I wonder how she is and what she's doing. I wonder as I look at all of these lights, is one of them her. Is she out there? Behind every one of these bright lights there's a story, and you've just read mine.

.

Aftermath

Jamal died three months after I completed this book. He died of prostate cancer in the prison hospital. He was 63 years old. Very little was known about Jamal and even less was spoken of him. He left behind the legacy of Al-Ossrah. Up until his death I would visit him every week. Once he found out he was terminally ill I became like his priest that he confessed to. Sometimes we just spoke about sports.

No one on the street knows the true story behind Momo and his involvement with the F.B.I.'s COINTELPRO but Gorgeous, Ben Diamond and myself. If you ask anyone on the streets of L.A. who killed Momo they will probably say Mustafa. Even though Mustafa knows it's not true, he has never denied it openly. In my opinion he enjoys the notoriety even if it's falsely given.

Al-Ossrah as a family remains intact and even more powerful today. They're more powerful now than they ever were mainly because of their international ties which Momo established with those overseas trips. Al-Ossrah passes information from one to another to protect its solidarity.
87% of all the worlds heroin comes from Afghanistan with 225,000 acres, 350 square miles of poppy fields. Momo's trips out of the country were to establish a worldwide Islamic connection from manufacture to distribution to wholesale to retail worldwide.

Poppy from Afghanistan, shipped to Syria and processed, then shipped to the US. Once received in the US the entire network is controlled by Al-Ossrah. Over the course of ten years he successfully connected eastern Islamic organized brotherhoods to the western Islamic organized brotherhoods to create one dynasty.

They met in a secret ceremony in Pakistan. They call it The Crescent Connection. The night of Momo's death he gave a sack full of money to Ali and the Afghan contact.

Ali lives in Pakistan as the overseas representative for Al-Ossrah. He makes sure that the poppy pipeline doesn't get interrupted.

After the deaths of its founders, Muhammad and Jamal, I would have thought Mustafa would have gotten the top spot of Sultan. But the Sheikhs unanimously voted against him. The main reason was because of that Black Mafia Hustler experiment, which has been dismantled and its members scattered. The new undisputed Sultan of l-Ossrah is a meek man of 5 feet 4 inches. Half black half Indonesian named Osiris. Osiris refuses to speak or write a written word. He only communicates through sign language.

Mustafa was allowed to live with a split decision secret ballot vote. He was demoted permanently to the rank of soldier. He is now required to kick in 50% of his record company profits directly to the family. Which still leaves him with a high eight figure a year income. He still remains the most visible of all Al-Ossrah members.

When Muhammad and I spoke in private, he personally proposed me for official membership in Al-Ossrah. But he was killed before he could do so. Right now the ranks are at 99. There are many in line, including myself. But you never really know. They approach you, you don't approach them. And you dare not refuse an invitation.

Benjamin Diamond is a man whom I have grown to have a great deal of respect for. We have actually become friends. He's like a mentor to me now in many ways as well as a surrogate grandfather to my son. What I know now, but I didn't know when I was writing this book is that Ben Diamond was a second-generation gangster. Ben's father, David Diamond, was a trusted lieutenant of famous L.A. gangster Mickey Cohen. Mickey Cohen later became right-hand man to the infamous gangster, Bugsy Siegel. The Siegel/Cohen Crime Family still exist today, based in San Jose California.

I see him about once a month now. He still owns and operates the Diamond Pawn Shop in

Watts, California. And he's still one of the biggest fences in that area and one of my best all-around resources. Every Monday he and I meet for coffee and conversation.

Lamont Carlson was arrested on narcotics charges. While awaiting trial, he was arrested on a separate charge, three counts of conspiracy to commit murder. He's looking at life and right now and being held without bail.

Tony Pleasure is currently working on an album deal for two of his artist. He recently signed a production contract with Mustafa's record company.

Hassan and Fatimah are still married. They have no children yet. I personally think Fatimah is unable to conceive, but I wouldn't dare mention it to her. I envy their relationship. Whenever I hear from them they seem so happy. I truly wish them the best. They shower Hussain with gifts. They really spoil him.

Aminah and I were not that lucky. Aminah gave birth to a healthy baby girl named Fatimah Bernadette Sharif. The stress of the new baby on top of all that had happened drove Aminah to her breaking point. Shortly after the birth of our daughter, Aminah and I got a divorce. I let her keep the house. All I took were my clothes and some pictures of our children.

THE ROYAL FAMILY;

Purrfect and Fantasy are in Atlanta, Georgia. They put their money together and they own an adult bookstore. We talk about once or twice a month. Word through the grapevine is that Purrfect is a madam down south with a thriving escort service. But I can't confirm that so I write that off as rumor.

Candy died before I finished this book. She died of an overdose due to excessive cocaine and heroin usage. The police discovered her body in a motel off Broadway. At the wake, I sent Cliff to give her mother a check for 50 grand.

Cleopatra manages Club Mae Westside, the club Lamont and I own together. But since Lamont's arrest, his aunt has taken over his interest in the club. The club is actually in his aunt's name. To make a long story short, she's trying to buy/push me out. When Lamont was the owner he would basically be gone. I would be upstairs in my office with the books and receipts and Cleopatra would work the floor. Now his aunt is in my office, Cleopatra's uncomfortably on the floor and I hardly show up. The way things are going now I'll probably let her buy me out and take Cleo with me, but who knows.

Baby Girl finished high school and is headed for college. For some reason, she comes by to visit me at my condo about three times a week. I think she's homesick and misses the excitement and comradery of The Royal Family. We sit, talk and usually just watch T.V. Sometimes she sits at the kitchen table across from me. She doesn't say a word, just sits there and does her homework. I sit across from her on my laptop and write books.

I never saw or heard from **Gorgeous** again.

Glossary

Please Google for more detailed definitions

After Hours- An illegal night club that usually operates out of a retail storefront as a cover. The term afterhours refer to the hours of operation which are 2am to 6am. Alcohol, drugs and prostitution are available on the premises. These underground clubs have no permits or liquor licenses.

As-Salaam Alaikum- Universal Muslim greeting in the Arabic language which means Peace Be Unto You.

Bloods- A street gang founded in Los Angeles with membership in the thousands. The gang is widely known for its rivalry with the Crips. They are identified by the red color worn by their members and by particular gang symbols, including distinctive hand signs. The Bloods are made up of various sub-groups known as "sets" between which significant differences exist such as colors, clothing, and operations, and political ideas which may be in open conflict with each other. Since their creation, the Blood gangs have branched out throughout the United States. Bloods have been documented in the US military, found in both US and overseas bases. Most notable members: T. Rodgers, Michael 'Harry-O' Harris and Suge Knight.

Black Panther- Term used for a member of The Black Panther Party.

Black Panther Party- An African American- revolutionary, left-wing organization working for the self-defense for black people. It was active in the United States from the mid-1960s into the 1970s. The Black Panther Party achieved national and international fame through their deep involvement in the Black Power movement and in

US politics of the 1960s and 70s. Today considered one of the most significant social, political and cultural currents in US History. Most notable members: Huey Newton, Bobby Seale, Fred Hampton, Jamil Al-Amin a.k.a. H.Rap Brown, Kwame Ture a.k.a Stokely Carmichael, & Bobby Rush who is currently a U.S. Congressmen.

Black P. Stone Nation- The largest Bloods gang on the west side of Los Angeles believed to have been started by infamous gangster T.Rodgers. The Black P. Stone Nation is said to have originated in Chicago and is an offshoot of the El-Rukns, but do not share their Islamic beliefs.

Caliph- Refers to a position held in Al-Ossrah equilivent to second in command answering only to the Sultan.

El-Rukns-A Chicago-based street gang estimated to have more than 20,000 members. The gang was originally formed in the late 1950s as a civil rights

organization called the Blackstone Rangers.
In later years, a quasi-Islamic faction of the gang emerged, naming themselves the El Rukn tribe of the Moorish Science Temple or simply El-Rukn. The Blackstone Rangers founder and religious leader is Prince Chief Abdullah Malik born Jeff Fort. The BPSN finances itself through a wide array of criminal activities and are part of the large Chicago gang alliance known as the People Nation.

LAPD- Los Angeles Police Department

Muslim Mafia- A term given by the American media for Islamic organized crime organizations or Jihadist organizations with an illegal GNP.

BGF- Black Guerrilla Family is a prison gang founded in 1966 by George Jackson while he was in the San Quentin State Prison. Originally the BGF was called the Black Family or the Black Vanguard and were associated with the Black Mafia. Some BGF members were formerly associated with the

Black Liberation Army, Symbionese Liberation Army and the Weatherman Underground Organization.

BLA- Black Liberation Army was an underground, black nationalist-Marxist militant organization that operated in the United States from 1970 to 1981. Composed largely of former Black Panthers, the organization's program was one of armed struggle and its stated goal was to take up arms for the liberation and self-determination of black people in the United States. The BLA carried out a series of bombings, robberies which they refer to as expropriations, and prison breaks. Most notable members: Assata Shakur, Geronimo Pratt and Mutulu Shakur (rapper Tupac Shakur's stepfather).

Sheikh- Refers to a position in Al-Ossrah equilivant to a lieutenant.

Southwest Jr. College- Community college located at 1600 West Imperial Hwy in Los Angeles, CA.

COINTELPRO- An acronym for **C**ounter **Intel**ligence **Pro**gram was a series of covert, and often illegal, projects conducted by the United States FBI aimed at investigating and disrupting dissident political organizations within the United States. The FBI stated motivation at the time was "protecting national security, preventing violence, and maintaining the existing social and political order."

Crips- A Los Angeles based street gang founded in 1971. With membership in the tens of thousands their primary source of income is derived from drug trafficking, robbery, extortion, murder for hire, grand larceny, burglary and identification theft. Most notable members: Raymond Washington, Stanley 'Tookie' Williams, Raymond Washington, Michael Conception and Monster Kody.

Sultan- Refers to a position in Al-Ossrah equal to king, supreme ruler.

Vietnam Vet- Refers to a soldier who served in the United States Armed Forces during the Vietnam Conflict.

Wa-Alaikum Salaam- Universal Muslim response to a greeting in the Arabic language which translates as peace be unto you too.

Work- Street vernacular which refers to murders committed and verified.

About The Author

Mickey Royal resides in Los Angeles, California where he is currently writing his next book. Contact Mickey Royal personally at;

Mickeyroyal2016@yahoo.com
Facebook (Mickey Royal)
mickeyroyal.com

Other books available by Mickey Royal At Amazon.com, Mickeyroyal.com or wherever books are sold.

Description

The Pimp Game:
Instructional Guide........................14.95
by Mickey Royal

The former Hollywood king reveals secret techniques with proven results on mastering the art of submission. A look inside the mind of the master as well as a chilling peek into the shadow world. A modern-day guide parallel to The Prince by Machiavelli.

Along For The Ride.........................14.95
by Mickey Royal

An autobiographical account of how Mickey Royal establishes The Royal Family; an organized stable of prostitutes, which runs with the efficiency of a Fortune 500 company. At the same time, this powerful family takes on crooked cops, overzealous music executives, drug lords and the Muslim Mafia to solve a six-year-old murder mystery.

Pimping Ain't Easy:
But Somebody's Gotta Do It..................14.95
by Mickey Royal

Coffee, a journalism student on spring break who has been given the assignment of a lifetime. She follows Mickey Royal around for seven days as she gathers intel for her mid-term. She soon finds herself entangled in the shadow world and embarks on an adventure she won't soon forget.

Other books available by Mickey Royal At Amazon.com, Mickeyroyal.com or wherever books are sold.

**I'm Leaving you
for a White Woman..........14.95**

Dennis, seeing no other way to solve the problems in his relationship seeks the counseling of a therapist. During his soul-searching excavation, he un-earths repressed feelings of emasculation and anxiety, due to decades of systematic subliminally subconscious emotional abuse at the hands of Black Women. Painstakingly arriving to the conclusion that many Black Men have. But until now, were afraid to come forward.